Help Wanted: Wife

Woman aged 30-40
Cooking and cleaning skills
very important
Must like children

Apply in person at the
Rocky T Ranch,
24 miles north of town
on Highway 10.

When Sylvie Smith read the printed notice on the supermarket bulletin board, she was desperate enough to apply. After all, she had a new baby and eight dollars left in her wallet.

The last thing she expected was to be met by a tall, sexy cowboy who didn't know a thing about the advertisement. Joe Brockett claimed he didn't want a wife! But oh, how she wanted to show him exactly how *good* married life could be....

Kristine Rolofson loves to write about the West. After living in north Idaho for twelve years before moving back to New England, she misses the small-town life of western towns and enjoys recreating that life in her novels for Harlequin.

A mother of six, Kristine also enjoys writing about women who attempt to do the right thing for their children, even against great odds and when the world—and especially old automobiles—conspire against them.

In her next life, Kristine wants to travel around the world and/or be a country-western singer, but don't tell her family that.

Books by Kristine Rolofson

HARLEQUIN TEMPTATION

Don't miss any of our special offers. Write to us at the following address for information on our newest releases.

Harlequin Reader Service
U.S.: 3010 Walden Ave., P.O. Box 1325, Buffalo, NY 14269
Canadian: P.O. Box 609, Fort Erie, Ont. L2A 5X3

Kristine Rolofson
THE RIGHT MAN IN MONTANA

HARLEQUIN®

TORONTO • NEW YORK • LONDON
AMSTERDAM • PARIS • SYDNEY • HAMBURG
STOCKHOLM • ATHENS • TOKYO • MILAN • MADRID
PRAGUE • WARSAW • BUDAPEST • AUCKLAND

ISBN 0-373-25812-7

THE RIGHT MAN IN MONTANA

Copyright © 1998 by Kristine Rolofson.

1

KAREN BROCKETT SURVEYED the crowded supermarket bulletin board and looked for a good spot. A spot she could reach. A spot sure to be noticed by the mothers coming in and out of Buttrey's. The *perfect* spot. She carefully handed four days of hard work to her little sister. "Don't drop them."

"I won't." Janie gripped the cards with mittened hands while Karen rearranged the bulletin board and Peter kicked a shopping cart with the toe of his boot. The eleven-year-old hesitated over an ad for free kittens—there were two white ones, and everybody knew white kittens were the smartest—before moving four business cards off to the side. No one was going to want their carpets cleaned right before Christmas and besides, their ad was the most important.

Janie shivered as the doors opened and a blast of cold air swept inside. Karen glanced toward the two women who walked past them to get shopping carts. *Too old.*

"You sure you're not gonna get in trouble?" the little girl asked.

"I'm sure," Karen replied, and her younger siblings knew better than to argue. "I put the boring stuff over here and made room in the middle. Okay, give me one.'' Janie obediently held out the card.

"Stupid," the little boy mumbled as he kicked at another shopping cart. "It's a stupid idea and you're—"

Karen shot him a warning look. "Don't call names."

"Can if I want to," he said, shoving his hands in his pockets. "Can we go home now?"

"Pretty soon."

"Can we look at the toys?"

"It's a *grocery* store, Pete," Karen said, sharing a red thumbtack from the business card of an insurance company with a corner of her blue card. "Not a toy store."

"They have toys," Janie dared to insist. "Not a whole lot, but some."

"Can I go look?"

"In a minute." She wanted to make sure this was exactly right.

"How many more days?"

"Ten." She didn't have to ask what he meant. He was only five and it was December. They were running out of time.

Peter sighed. "That's a lot." He frowned up at his big sister. "Are you sure this is gonna work?"

"I hope so." Karen stepped back and studied her work. She'd used the computer at school and made a special heading in bold print. An attention getter, that was for sure. And better than writing it by hand and having it look like it was done by a kid.

"Where's Uncle Joe?"

"At the café." She'd told her uncle they had Christmas shopping to do, and he'd been too busy talking to the waitress to see his niece tape a piece of blue paper to the window that held all the other important announcements. "We'll go back soon."

Janie stamped her feet. "My toes are cold."

"Okay. Come on." Karen took the remaining two cards from her sister and then grabbed Peter's bare hand. "Did you lose your mittens again?"

"They're in my pocket."

She led the kids around the store until they found the aisle that had an assortment of baseball cards, action figures and puzzles. "You can look at the toys," she said, "but we're not buying any."

"Santa's coming," Janie said. "Isn't he?"

"Sure he is." If Uncle Joe remembered to send in the catalog order in time. Karen wished she were four years old again and still believed in Santa Claus. It would be a lot easier than being the oldest and always having to be the boss and worrying about everything.

She let the little kids check out the toys for a precious four minutes before tugging them toward the door. The front of the store was crowded with women waiting in the checkout lines, their carts piled high with food and wrapping paper and other special things that made

Christmas so pretty. Maybe she could talk Uncle Joe into coming back here and buying candy canes.

"Did our mommy make cookies?" Janie asked.

"Yes," Karen said, though it was getting harder and harder to remember those years. "Lots and lots. With green sugar and silver candy balls stuck on top."

"Wow."

She stopped before leaving the store, just to see if anyone was reading their ad yet, but that corner of the entry was empty. Karen blinked at the sudden stinging behind her eyes. She never cried. Never, ever. Crying was for babies, and everyone knew that Karen Brockett was all grown up. No one even asked her what she wanted for Christmas anymore. Which was why she had to get it all by herself.

"THE BIGGEST FOOL IN ALL of the universe is sitting right here in a parking lot in Montana," Sylvie Smith told her son. The baby didn't pay a bit of attention. Why would he, when he was busy having a late lunch? She shouldn't be sitting in a rapidly cooling Mazda talking to herself. Anyone who passed by would think she was half crazy, and maybe they would be right—especially if the past week was any indication.

She could blame her behavior on postpartum depression. She could say that she talked to herself because that was what single mothers did when there is no one else to listen. She could blame a December trip to Willum, Montana, on a desperate case of foolish optimism. She could explain that she'd hoped for another miracle to follow the miracle of childbirth, but she doubted that anyone would understand.

"This is what happens when Mommy gets greedy," she told her son, making sure every inch of him was snug against the cold, tucked inside her worn ski jacket, while he finished nursing. "Or this is what happens when mommies lose their jobs and run out of money."

Oh, not quite out of money. She had enough cash left for a motel room and food, if she was frugal. There was gas money to get back home, but no job and no home to get back to. She'd pinned her hopes on finding a new home in Willum, a small town that most people had never heard of, smack-dab in the middle of Montana. And her luck had run out.

"This is what happens," she murmured, shivering a little as the wind whipped around the car, "when mommies believe what daddies tell them."

Sylvie's stomach growled, reminding her that nursing mothers—insane or not—had to keep up their strength. She would buy some groceries and make her way back to that motel she'd spotted on the other side of town. It wouldn't do any good to feel sorry for herself, but then again, it was crystal clear that this wasn't a good week to waste money on lottery tickets.

"Come on, sweet pea," she told the sleeping baby. "Let's go shopping." Sylvie wiped his chin with a tissue, rearranged her clothing and pasted a confident smile on her face before getting out of the car. She huddled over the baby, keeping the blanket over his face, until she was inside the supermarket. Overheated and bright, it was a welcome change from the car. Sylvie bundled little Dillon into a shopping cart and, smelling fresh coffee, decided to treat herself to a cup and five minutes of pretending that life was normal again. The sign in front of the carafe said Help Yourself, so Sylvie did exactly that. She sat down in one of two plastic chairs and, making sure that Dillon was not in a draft, sipped the hot liquid and tried to figure out what she was going to do with the rest of her life.

When that became too depressing, she watched the people who entered the store. There were preoccupied men, women with lists and children, three rowdy teenagers, and two elderly ladies who clung together as if holding each other up. The teenagers examined a nearby community bulletin board and then giggled loud enough to wake Dillon.

"Do you see this one? My mom would really think this was funny."

"I need a job, but I don't need a job *that* bad."

"I think it's pretty cool," another said. "Like in a book."

"Jessie, you're an idiot," the tall one added, snapping her gum. "Nobody's that desperate. Hey, look! Kittens! Think my mom would let me get one?"

Sylvie stood to comfort Dillon, who went right back to sleep when the girls lost interest in the bulletin board and wandered away. "Good boy," she whispered, readjusting the thick blanket before turning to the bulletin board to see what job advertisement had amused the teenagers. It was there, in the center of the board, neatly typed on a blue card.

It had to be a joke. Sylvie read the words carefully, waiting for a punch line. No, it seemed serious enough. Concise. Direct. She'd heard of these kinds of things before. There had been a Texas billionaire on *Oprah*, and the man who had rented a billboard. She'd heard people advertised. To be fair, she supposed it wasn't much different than putting an ad in the Personals column of the newspaper.

"Nobody's that desperate." Wasn't that what one of the teenage girls had said? "Desperate" was sitting in a supermarket in a strange town and being grateful for a free cup of coffee. "Desperate" was wanting your child to have a father and not being able to find him. "Desperate" was talking to yourself in front of a bulletin board. Sylvie leaned closer and read it again.

Woman, age thirty to forty. Sylvie pretended to consider whether or not she was qualified for the job. She'd be thirty in a few months.

Cooking and cleaning skills very important. Which meant he was a practical man who liked his meals hot and his house clean. Yes, she could cook and clean. She'd been doing it since she was twelve.

Must like children. That was easy, she thought, glancing toward Dillon. Obviously the man who'd placed this ad had a child of his own. And he cared about that child.

Experience preferred, but not necessary. Sylvie thought of Dillon's father and the months they'd spent together. Did that make her experienced for this job? No comment.

Apply in person at the Rocky T Ranch, twenty-four miles north of town on Highway 10. She didn't know where Highway 10 was, but she had a map of Montana out in the car.

She wasn't considering this job, she told herself, dropping the empty cardboard cup into a nearby garbage can. She hoisted the strap of her handbag over her shoulder and pushed her shopping cart away from the bulletin board's ridiculous plea. She would buy some disposable diapers, peanut butter, bread and milk. Maybe she'd splurge on a couple of oranges if they were cheap enough. Sylvie waited in the lengthy checkout line while Dillon, who wanted his diaper changed, screamed loud enough to drown out "Jingle Bells" on the loudspeaker.

"The little darlings get tired, don't they," said an elderly woman with a kind smile.

"Yes, they sure do." Sylvie tried not to look pathetic.

"He sounds real worn-out, but he'll be fine once you get him home and settled in his own bed."

"Yes," was all Sylvie could answer before the woman turned back to the cashier to write a check for her groceries. She rocked Dillon in her arms and waited to pay for her food. Yes, the baby would be better when he was settled in for the night. But Dillon didn't have a home, and his bed was a padded playpen she'd bought at a Salvation Army shop. All along she'd thought that Dillon would have a father, only she'd been wrong. She would survive, but her son would be the one to suffer the most.

Sylvie managed to pay for her groceries without dropping the baby or having a nervous breakdown—an accomplishment she promised herself she'd celebrate later. She made it through the automatic door and into the parking lot before she hesitated. She could return to the car, return to a very uncertain future.

Or not.

The sky had grown dark since she'd been inside the store. Snowflakes stung her face—reminders that Montana weather could be harsh and unforgiving to travelers. It was time, long past time, to be sensible. And practical. Sylvie took a deep breath and trudged back into the supermarket. She'd promised her son a father and she was damn well going to try to get him one. And in time for Christmas, too.

The blue card was still there, its bold plea shouting at Sylvie from ten feet away. Help Wanted: Wife.

JOE BROCKETT WAS OF TWO minds when it came to Saturdays. He sure enjoyed the weekly trip to town, liked meeting up with friends at the diner, didn't even mind going to the bank before noon and taking care of business at the feed store. But Saturday days led to Saturday nights, and if a rancher got lonely once in a while, it was sure to happen on a Saturday night.

He wished he could remember the days when he'd been young and wild and full of hell on a Saturday night, but if he'd ever had any wild Saturday nights, he sure couldn't remember them. Joe opened the refrigerator and peered inside for inspiration.

"Chili," he said, only to be greeted by identical expressions of distaste. "What's wrong with chili?"

Karen sighed as if she figured her uncle was mentally deficient. "You gave us chili on Wednesday and Thursday and Friday. And I don't like what it does to my tummy."

"Oh." The three kids sat at the old oak table, a worn deck of Uno cards in front of them. He had to hand it to them: They sure knew how to amuse themselves. "Any ideas?"

Peter looked up and grinned. "Let's have breakfast for dinner."

"Again?"

The three of them nodded. "Uno," Peter crowed, slapping down a card.

"Breakfast it is," Joe declared, pulling out a bowl of eggs and a container of milk. "I'll fry up some bacon, too."

"Bacon's bad for you," Karen said. "Has too much ch'lesterol."

"Where do you learn this stuff?"

"School. Mrs. McGuire says we shouldn't eat too much fat."

Mrs. McGuire could come over and cook dinner then, Joe figured, rummaging through the lower shelf of the refrigerator. He found the package of bacon and set it out on the counter next to the eggs. "I'll drain it on paper towels," he promised, hoping that would satisfy Mrs. McGuire *and* his fussy niece.

Peter pushed the cards to the center of the table. "Can we get the tree tomorrow? You said we could."

"Yeah, well, I'll try." He supposed they could get it over with. He didn't have much choice.

"It's almost Christmas," the boy informed him. "Ten days, Karen said."

"That's right. Ten days." And Karen was never wrong. The child was old beyond her years, but there wasn't a whole lot he could do to change that.

Janie appeared at his elbow. "Pancakes or French toast?"

"French toast," he said, hoping that was the right answer. Janie had her mother's smile, but she didn't use it often enough. This time the little girl smiled, so Joe let out a sigh of relief. "You want to help me?"

"Can I break the eggs?"

"Sure." Which would mean a mess, but what the hell. There'd be bacon grease and syrup everywhere anyway, but he had all night to clean it up and nothing better to do. Janie dragged a chair over to the counter and climbed up on it.

"Just four eggs, Janie, that's all." He took what he hoped was a clean bowl from the overhead cabinet. "Put 'em in here."

"Somebody's coming!" Karen said, peering out the window. "Cookie's barking and I can see lights."

Joe poured a generous amount of milk into the bowl. "Where is that dog, anyway?"

"On the front porch," Peter said, running over to the side window. "Who's comin', Uncle Joe?"

"Beats me. No one should be driving out here in a storm. Honey, don't drop the shells—" Too late. They'd be crunching their French toast tonight unless he could fish the pieces of eggshell out of there. With any luck they'd sink to the bottom. "Maybe your grandfather's stopping in on his way home from town."

"Uh-uh," Karen said, her face glued to the window. "It's not a truck."

"No?"

"It's a lady."

That got his attention. Joe gave Janie the mixing spoon and joined Karen at the window. "Anyone you recognize?"

"No." Karen could barely hide her excitement. "It's a stranger."

"What the he—heck would a stranger be doing out here this time of day?" He went to the back door and peered out. Sure enough, a woman stood beside her small car. She held something in her arms, but the winter sky had darkened so that Joe couldn't see much except shapes. "Maybe she's lost. Pete, go tell Grandpa's dog to shut up."

The little boy hesitated. "I'm not supposed to say 'shut up.'"

"Tell him to be quiet, then."

"Can I see?" Janie wriggled past him and stood in the door.

"Hello!" Joe called, but the wind blew his words away. "Hello!" he tried, louder this time, and the woman hurried across the yard toward the house. Joe remembered to flick on the switch for the outside floodlight so his guest could find the snow-crusted path to the back door. The wind blew snow against his face, stinging his skin and making him blink.

"Who do you think she is?" Karen slid under his arm to watch the woman.

"I don't have any idea, but I do know she's going to fall if she isn't careful." Joe went outside to help her. He barely noticed that the wind had picked up, and the temperature had lowered a few degrees. "Let me help you with that," he said when he reached her. "And watch your step."

Her head was ducked down against the wind, but wisps of blond hair blew out from under the jacket's hood. He was glad that she wore practical, rubber-soled boots; not so pleased when he saw that she carried what looked like a baby in her arms. Joe swallowed a curse and ushered the woman inside. She stood amid the clutter and readjusted the weight in her arms. She must be lost, and the last thing needed at the Rocky T was another problem.

"Come on in where it's warm," Joe said.

"You have a baby?" Karen asked, leaning forward to see.

"Let the woman in the house." His words came out more sternly than he'd intended, but everyone moved into the kitchen without any further conversation. The three children stood back and eyed the visitor with something that looked like awe.

"Yes, this is Dillon," the woman said in so soft a voice that the children had to lean forward to catch the words. She unwrapped the blanket to expose a tiny face.

Peter gulped. "Is he dead?"

"No. Just asleep." She tickled the corner of the baby's mouth and his lips turned up in a tiny smile. "See?"

Joe waited for her to explain what she was doing here, but the woman looked at him as if waiting for him to say something. "Uh, can I help you with something?"

"I came about the ad," she said, raising her chin to look at him as if she thought he was about to pounce.

"The ad," he repeated, wishing he knew what she was talking about. "What—"

"Fire!" Karen yelped, pointing to the stove. "The bacon's on fire!"

Joe jumped and was halfway across the room before he realized there were no flames coming from the pan. A little smoke, but nothing worse.

"It's only smoke," he said. "You guys always ask for crunchy bacon."

"Oh, I thought I saw some flames shooting up." Karen's cheeks were flushed and her brown eyes were wide. Did she think he was going to get upset over burned food?

"Don't worry about it," he said, turning the burner off. Getting his unexpected guest to where she needed to go might take a while.

He motioned to a kitchen chair. "Why don't you sit down?" Though he didn't know what he was going to say.

"Thank you." She sat down and, tucking the baby in the crook of her left arm, managed to push her hood off her hair and lower the jacket's zipper by a few inches. Pale yellow hair tumbled to her shoulders, making her look impossibly young. Joe's heart sank, but the children drew nearer to her as if fascinated.

"Karen?"

The girl looked over at him. She was very pale. "You okay?"

"Sure," she said, but she dropped her gaze and stayed close to the woman. "What's your name?"

"Sylvia," the woman replied. "But my friends call me 'Sylvie.'"

Joe sat down and fixed his chair so he faced her. "I'm Joe Brockett. This is my niece, Karen," he said, nodding toward the older girl, "and over there are Janie and Peter."

"Hello," she said, smiling at each one. "I'm happy to meet you." Her smile faded when she turned back to Joe and the look in those blue eyes held terror. He didn't know what to do to ease her nerves. "I've never done anything like this before."

So that was it. The poor woman had never been lost. "Well, I have," he said, hoping to make her relax. "We've been through this a number of times."

The color drained out of Sylvie Smith's skin. "A number of times?" she repeated.

"Sure," he said, wondering why she looked as if she might pass out.

She took a deep breath. "I can cook and clean." When he didn't say anything, she added, "You said in the ad that cooking and cleaning were very important."

"I really think—"

She interrupted him, as if she had to get the words out. "And I've had…a lot of experience with taking care of children."

"Well, that's good, I guess, but I don't know what the hell—excuse me—this has to do with me."

Those blue eyes couldn't get any wider, he thought. She was almost pretty, or she might be if she cleaned up a little. There were dark circles under her eyes. She wore no makeup, no lipstick, no jewelry. He couldn't tell if she was married or not because she hadn't taken off her gloves. "Isn't this the Rocky T Ranch? I'm sure I followed the directions."

"Yeah, but I don't know anything about an ad." The room grew silent. Too silent. The young woman pulled a piece of paper out of her pocket and with a shaking hand gave it to him.

"Is there someone else who lives here who might have written this? I saw this at the supermarket in town this afternoon."

Joe took the paper and glanced toward his older niece. A guilty flush spread over her cheeks and she wouldn't meet his gaze. "This afternoon?"

"Yes," the woman—Sylvia Something—said. "It was on the bulletin board."

Joe looked down at the blue paper. Help Wanted: Wife. "Oh, hell," he said, turning to Karen. "What in the world goes through your head?"

"Maybe Grandpa did it."

Hank Cavendish might be a pain in the ass sometimes, but the old man wouldn't advertise for a wife in a supermarket; at the Playhouse Bar, maybe. "Let's find out. Get him on the phone for me."

Karen ignored him and leaned over Sylvie's snow-covered shoulder. "You want me to put your jacket by the stove? It'll get warm that way."

"I think I'd better be going." The woman stood and looked as if she was blinking back tears. *Tears?*

"Just a minute," Joe said, holding up one hand as if to stop everyone from going anywhere. And it worked, because the woman sank back into the chair. "You came out here to answer an ad to be a *wife?*"

"I know it sounds a little odd, but—"

"A little *odd?* You don't even know me. You could have walked into a real dangerous situation, lady." No wonder she looked as if she was going to faint. The idiotic woman thought she was selling herself to a stranger.

"I know, but it's been a pretty bad week and—"

"Wait a minute." He read the rest of the advertisement before turning to Karen again. "Tell the truth. This was your idea?"

"We need help. Even Grandpa said—"

"Don't start, Karen. You're in big trouble this time."

"But—"

"But nothing. You've played a mean trick on this lady and you're going to be punished." He was about ready to burst with frustration, especially since his niece looked anything but contrite.

"Can she stay for supper? After all, she's *company*," Karen insisted.

"Brought here on false pretenses," he reminded his niece.

Janie frowned. "What's that?"

"Some kinda car," Peter said.

"Please stay for supper," Karen offered, leaning against Sylvie's chair. "Uncle Joe doesn't really mean to yell."

"At least let me give you something to eat," Joe said, remembering his manners, though he didn't know what to do. "It's the least I can do after what these kids have pulled." He watched her take a deep breath. "How about a cup of coffee?"

"I'd like that," the woman said, her blue eyes shimmering with unshed tears. "This is so embarrassing."

"Give me your jacket," Karen said.

Janie leaned over the table. "Can I hold the baby?"

Joe put up a warning hand. "Quiet, all of you." He turned to the woman and held out his arms. "I'll hold the baby while you get your coat off."

She hesitated, obviously debating whether or not she could trust him to hold that baby, then leaned forward and reluctantly handed him the sleeping child.

"I've held kids before," he assured her, carefully cradling the infant in his arms. The little boy didn't waken, though his eyelids flickered a couple of times. Joe turned his attention back to the child's mother and watched as she shrugged out of a coat that had seen better days. She wore a blue sweater and faded jeans, and her hands were bare of rings. He noticed how delicate she was; in fact, she looked like she'd blow over from the first strong wind. "Where are you from?"

"I don't live around here," she said, taking back the baby. Her fingers grazed his shirt-sleeves—a touch of warmth that made Joe flinch with surprise before he released his hold on the child. "The fact is, I answered your ad because—"

Her words were cut off by the baby's cry. The infant began to wail as if he were being tortured.

"What the hell is the matter with him?"

"He's hungry," she said, looking awfully calm for someone holding a child in pain. She smiled a little at Joe's expression. "He always does this. Just wakes up screaming for food."

"You want me to get something from your car?" He stood, ready to do whatever was needed to help.

"No." Her pale cheeks turned pink. "I have everything I need. If I could go someplace quiet with him…"

"Oh," he said, suddenly realizing what she meant. "Sure. Janie, take Sylvie into the living room."

"Sure. Come on, Sylvie," she said, taking the woman's hand. "I'll show you the most bestest chair."

"Thank you," the woman replied, allowing herself to be led into the living room. When they disappeared down the hall, Joe turned to the remaining children.

"I'll deal with you in a minute," he told Karen. "But for now I guess we'd better get supper going," he said, going over to the stove. "Karen, you beat up those eggs. Pete, you set the table."

"For how many?"

He took the plates from the cupboard and set them down on the counter, then he turned the heat on underneath the cast-iron skillet. "Five.

"She's staying?" Karen looked as excited as if tomorrow was Christmas morning.

"Only for supper," he said. "And you're going to apologize to her, too. Pour her a cup of coffee and take it in to her, see if she wants it now."

Karen didn't look as if she minded. "Okay."

"And you're in big trouble."

The kid had the nerve to smile.

"I mean it," he insisted. "You can't do weird stuff like this. Nobody gets a wife from advertising. It just doesn't work that way." He watched as Karen poured coffee into her mother's favorite china cup. "I told you, I'm not the kind of guy that gets married."

"Yes, Uncle Joe, I know." She hurried into the living room, leaving Joe alone with his nephew and his frying pan. He'd been ready to get married once, and only once. After that, he'd decided he was better off being single, just in case she ever needed him. That was a long time ago, but Joe had no intention of getting involved that way again.

So why did he feel like he'd been punched in the gut?

2

SHE'D THOUGHT SHE WAS going to faint, she really did. If Dillon hadn't cried and given her an excuse to leave the room, she might have collapsed right there in the overheated kitchen. The air in the large living room seemed cooler, but maybe that was because the man who didn't want a wife wasn't in here with her. Sylvie avoided the obviously masculine recliner and sank onto the couch instead. She rearranged her clothing and soothed her screaming son by putting him to her breast, then quickly covered herself with his blanket. All the while, Janie watched her with a fascinated expression.

"Should you go help with dinner?" Sylvie wanted nothing more than to be left alone so she could close her eyes and think about what to do next. Obviously, marriage was no longer an option. She thought of the horrified expression on Mr. Brockett's face and didn't know whether to laugh or cry. He thought she was crazy and she knew it would take more energy than she had left to try to explain.

"We're getting a Christmas tree," the little girl confided, ignoring the question about helping.

She climbed onto the couch and knelt close to Sylvie.

"That sounds like fun. Where are you going to put it?" Sylvie glanced around a room that held a mix of styles, from a polished antique rocking chair to upholstered chairs slipcovered in faded chintz. Ivory walls held family photographs and stuffed, mounted fish. There were no signs that Christmas was less than two weeks away. A comfortable clutter of pillows, magazines, toys and newspapers lay scattered on the pine floor.

Janie pointed to a bank of windows across the room. "Over there."

"That's a good spot," Sylvie agreed. She wished she could kick off her damp boots and curl up under the quilt that someone had left in a heap in the corner of the couch. "You have a very nice house."

Karen tiptoed into the room and put a cup of coffee under a brass lamp on the end table. "I'm supposed to say I'm sorry."

"Are you?"

The older girl sighed. "I guess."

Not exactly filled with guilt, Sylvie noted. "Thank you for the coffee."

"Sure." The child didn't move. "Do you need anything else?"

Dillon's father. A warm bed. A job. A good night's sleep. "No, thank you, Karen."

"I can get milk and sugar for your coffee," she offered.

"I drink it black, but thank you for asking."

She didn't dare try to drink it while nursing Dillon, so she contented herself with the aroma.

"I'm in trouble," Karen said.

"You should be," Sylvie said gently. "You put your father and me in a very embarrassing situation."

"He's not my father." Karen sat down on the floor by Sylvie's feet.

"No?" Good heavens, what had she gotten herself into, here? Sylvie wondered if she should stand right now and, with Dillon attached, grab her things and head for the car.

"He's our uncle," Karen explained, sounding a little sad.

"Mommy and Daddy died," Janie said. "Want to know what I want for Christmas?"

Sylvie nodded, trying to digest Janie's matter-of-fact statement.

"Two baby dolls and a pony."

"A real pony?" She adjusted the blanket and noticed that her son had fallen asleep once again, after finishing only half of his meal. He would waken in two hours and act as if she hadn't fed him in a week.

Janie giggled. "Yep. A *little* pony."

She would leave here as soon as possible, before the snow got any worse. Plan B: Find that cheap motel and make a peanut-butter sandwich. Tomorrow she'd buy a paper and look for work. And maybe she shouldn't stop looking for Billy Ray. Just because she'd had no luck before didn't mean it would always be that way.

"Uncle Joe is making supper," Karen said. "Bacon and eggs."

"And French toast," Janie added.

"He makes really good breakfast. That's why we have it for supper." Karen leaned forward and lowered her voice. "He doesn't cook too good most of the time."

Janie pointed to the fieldstone fireplace that took up most of the far wall. "Santa comes down the chimney."

Karen rolled her eyes. "That's all she talks about. Santa, Santa, Santa."

"I *love* him," her younger sister said. "He's gonna bring me a pony."

Sylvie adjusted her sweater, then lifted Dillon to her shoulder and patted his back until he burped, making a quiet little sound against her neck. "I think we'd better be going," she told the girls.

Janie scrambled down from the couch and stood next to her sister. "You can't go," Karen said. "Not yet."

"I have to." She tucked Dillon against her left side and used her free hand to rummage through the diaper bag for a clean diaper. She might as well change him now. It would be an even longer ride back to town if Dillon started crying again.

"You're not staying for supper?"

"I can't." She protected the couch with a small pad, then hurried through the diaper changing, all the while hoping her son wouldn't waken and protest. "There," she said, smiling at the girls. "Would you watch him while I go wash my hands?"

"Sure," the older girl said, sitting between the baby and the edge of the couch. "The bathroom's that way." She pointed toward the hall, so Sylvie hurried down the narrow corridor and found the bathroom. She didn't start crying until after she'd locked the door behind her. Oh, she hadn't meant to, but there was something about being alone all of a sudden that triggered tears. She folded the wet diaper and put it in the trash basket by the toilet, then washed her hands, all the while trying to choke back tears. Sylvie splashed cold water on her face and took deep, ragged breaths. She didn't dare look at herself in the mirror above the sink. She knew what she'd see: a woman who looked older than twenty-nine. A woman with pale skin and dark circles under her eyes. A woman who would be an ideal candidate for one of those makeover contests on *Live with Regis and Kathie Lee*.

She took a paper towel from the roll on the counter and dried her face and hands. No, she didn't need a makeover. She needed to either find or forget Billy Ray and, either way, get on with her life. There would be no more tears for Sylvie Smith.

"HEARD YOU'RE LOOKING for a wife." Ruby Dee put her hands on ample hips and pirouetted in front of Hank's barstool. "How 'bout me, Hank?"

Hank Cavendish chuckled. "Who said I was

looking for a wife, Ruby?" He took another swallow of beer, trying to make the one bottle he allowed himself to last for as long as possible. The annual Christmas party at the Playhouse Bar was in full swing already, and it wasn't even six o'clock yet. Ruby perched on the stool next to his, so Hank swiveled to face her.

"The sign in the window of the café," the bartender said. He jerked his chin toward the beer. "You want another one of those?"

"Nope. Thanks. What sign?"

"Tell him, Ruby."

"Clear as day, a sign that said someone at the Rocky T needs a wife. If it's not you," Ruby said, tapping her foot in time to the music, "then whoever's thinking about marriage must be Joe. You're the only two up there, right?"

"Couldn't be Joe," Hank declared. "He isn't looking to settle down."

"He should," Ruby said. "Lord knows, those little kids need a mother." She was a pretty good-looking woman, Hank noticed, not for the first time. Her gray-blond curls framed a damned attractive pair of blue eyes.

"Ol' Joe's a good boy. He works too hard, that's all." Hank turned away from the twinkle in those eyes to look at the band, a bunch of local boys who could play honky-tonk like no one else in the county, and didn't give the sign another thought. Somebody had made a mistake, that was all. He and Joe would have a few laughs about it later on.

"You want to dance, Hank?" Ruby asked.

He shook his head. "Me? Naw. At my age I'd have a heart attack or something."

"You're not that old," she chided. "And I know how to do CPR."

She couldn't be flirting with him, Hank thought. A woman like that, at least ten years younger than him and full of pep, wouldn't be flirting with a broken-down rancher. "Maybe next time," he drawled, finishing off the rest of his drink. "I'd better get back."

"Sure," she said. "Next time."

He would have sworn she looked disappointed, but that didn't make any sense. Ruby could have any man in town, but though she liked to be social on a Saturday night, everyone knew she didn't hook up with anyone when the bar closed. She ran the town's beauty parlor, and rumor was she'd been married more than once. She lived alone now, just like him.

"Gotta go," he said. He stood and pulled out his wallet. "I hear it's snowing pretty good out there now."

Ruby picked up her glass. "Merry Christmas, Hank."

"Yeah. Same to you, Ruby." Suddenly embarrassed, Hank tossed a ten onto the bar. "For me and the lady," he said, and strode away before Ruby could thank him. Fifteen minutes later he pushed his Patsy Cline cassette into the tape player and sang along. Laura had always said he had a good voice. She'd never given up trying to get him to go to church and join the choir. "I'm still singing," he told her.

He'd never given up talking to his wife, though she'd been gone eight years now. Most times it felt like eight days. He missed her. He sang along with Patsy while the snow blasted the truck's windshield. Tough night to be battling the weather, he figured, checking to make sure the truck was in four-wheel drive. Good night to be home in bed before the drifts piled up.

He and Joe would have their work cut out for them if this storm continued. A couple of the guys said they'd heard it was gonna be a big one, but someone always said that every time one little flake of snow blew across the plains.

Hank chuckled to himself at the thought of Joe putting up an ad for a wife. Why, he'd never heard of anything so funny in all his sixty-five years.

"WHERE IS SHE?"

"In the bathroom," Karen said, sitting beside the baby as if she were guarding it from a pack of wolves. Janie sat on the floor and rested her chin against a couch cushion. "Washing up."

"How's he doing?" Joe eyed the tiny baby, who waved his fists in the air and stared at Karen with blue eyes that matched his mother's. He was a cute little thing, if you liked babies. Which he wasn't sure he did.

"Great." Karen touched his fat little cheek. "Isn't he cute?"

"Yeah, sure." He glanced toward the hall and saw no sign of the baby's mother. He hoped she wasn't stealing him blind. She could be a con artist, a thief, an insane homeless woman who went around Montana answering strange advertisements. "How long has, uh, Sylvie been in the bathroom?"

"Just a few minutes. She changed Dillon's diaper and had to wash her hands."

At least the crazy woman was clean. He put his hands on his hips. "Karen, you and I have to have a talk."

"I can't right now," she said, not taking her gaze from the baby. "I'm baby-sitting."

"Don't get smart with me, young lady."

Janie looked up. "I love babies. Santa's gonna bring me two of 'em."

"Two?" Joe frowned. He thought he'd only ordered one, a hideous plastic baby with an oversize head and a bottle with disappearing "milk."

"And a pony."

Joe decided not to comment. Santa could take all the blame on Christmas morning when there wasn't an extra horse under the tree. "Supper's almost ready. You and I will talk later," he told his older niece. "You've got some explaining to do."

"Don't be too upset with her," Sylvie said as she entered the room. She walked past him and sat beside Karen. "There's no harm done and she's apologized."

Once again he was amazed by how young she looked. "How old are you?"

Her eyebrows rose, but she answered the question. "Twenty-nine."

"You shouldn't be looking for a husband, lady. You should be looking for a job."

"My goodness," she said, her blue eyes sparking. "Why didn't I think of that?"

"Supper's ready if you'd like to join us."

"Thanks, but no thanks." She started stuffing baby things into the backpack.

"You might as well have something to eat." For all he knew, she could be broke and hungry. In fact, she probably was.

"I have groceries in the car. I'll eat when I get to the motel."

"That's a long ride."

She shrugged and began to wrap the baby in his blanket. "We'll make it."

Okay, that was that. He shouldn't feel like a jerk. He was the one who'd been home frying bacon, not looking for trouble, just minding his own business. He didn't have to feel bad because this strange woman and her baby were about to leave the Rocky T and head into the night.

"You want your coffee?" Karen picked up the cup and held it out to Sylvie, who took it with a smile for the girl.

"I forgot," she said, taking a polite sip before setting it back on the table. "Thank you." She scooped the baby into her arms, slung the bag over her shoulder and stood. "All I need is my coat."

Janie scrambled up from the floor. "You can't have it!"

"What?"

The child shook her head. "Karen took it and we're not gonna give it back."

Enough was enough. Joe gave Karen his sternest look. "Get the lady's coat. *Now.*"

Karen burst into tears. "Doesn't anyone ever ask me what *I* want for Christmas?" She ran out of the room. Joe heard her rapid footsteps on the stairs, then the door to her bedroom slammed shut with a loud bang.

Sylvie looked as if she was going to cry, too. "It's not usually like this," he said, though he didn't think she'd believe him. "I'll find your coat."

"Okay."

"I don't know what's gotten into her lately. I'll be glad when Christmas is over."

She followed him into the kitchen, Janie trailing behind her like a lost lamb. Smoke wafted to the ceiling as bacon sizzled in the skillet.

"Anyone seen Sylvie's coat?"

Peter didn't look up from a game of solitaire. "Nope."

"Where did Karen put it?"

He shrugged. "The closet?"

Joe figured that would be too obvious and, after a search of the coat closet, knew he was right. He went through the hooks on the back porch, checking to see if Sylvie's worn parka was hidden under a barn jacket or a rain slicker. He muttered another apology to Sylvie and headed upstairs to confront his niece.

"Tell me where the jacket is," he called through the door.

"I don't want her to go," she sobbed. "It's not fair."

He wriggled the doorknob. The darn kid had locked him out. "What's not fair?"

Silence. Then the sound of Karen blowing her nose. "Everyone has a mother but me. Lindsey's mom takes her shopping and Becky's mom let her bake cookies for the whole class and Leigh's mom is really pretty and lets Leigh wear her rodeo shirt to school."

Oh, hell. Joe rested his shoulder against the door. "You wrote that ad because you wanted a mother?"

"It's the only way I'm gonna get one. And it *worked*, too, 'cept now you're sending her away."

"What did you think I was going to do, Karen? Marry the first woman who walked in the door?" He didn't understand girls. He didn't understand women. Aside from his mother, he'd only loved one woman in thirty-five years and he figured he'd go on loving her, too. She'd been worth it.

"I thought you'd meet someone and it would be like...magic," she sniffed.

"Open the door."

"No. You'll yell."

He took a deep breath and lied, "No, I won't." And then realized that he wasn't alone.

"I found it," Sylvie said, the baby tucked in her arms as she paused on the landing. She wore the old jacket, probably figuring if she didn't put it on right away, one of the kids would steal it again.

He wondered how much she'd heard. "Where?"

"In the clothes dryer. Can I talk to her?"

"She won't open the door."

"That's okay."

Easy for her to say. She'd be out of here in five minutes. He moved away from the door, but stayed close by.

"Karen?" Sylvie knocked on the door. "I found my coat and I didn't want to leave without saying goodbye."

They heard the key scratching in the lock, then Karen opened the door and peeked out. "You really have to go?"

"Oh, yes."

"But you don't have anywhere to live."

"Of course I do. I'm going to stay at the Daylight Motel, right there in Willum, and tomorrow Dillon and I will head back to Nebraska."

"That motel doesn't look very nice," the child said, daring a glance at her uncle. Joe didn't fall for the silent plea.

"Say goodbye, Karen," he told her. "The lady has to get going."

"Bye," she said, opening the door wide. She took a step forward to peek at the baby. "Bye, Dillon." When she would have joined them in the hall, Joe put up his hand.

"Might be a good idea for you to stay in your room for a while," he said. "I'll deal with you later."

"Okay," she said with a sigh, and turned to Sylvie. "I'll wave from my window."

"I'll wave back," she promised before Joe motioned her toward the stairs. He was five minutes away from the end of this embarrassing incident, thirty minutes from tucking the delinquents into bed, an hour from making one last check of that sick heifer in the barn. And a long two hours from downing a glass of Jack Daniel's and crawling into his own bed.

"Well," he said, after following her into the kitchen, "I'm real sorry about all this."

"No problem," she said, her smile firmly in place. She slung her bag over her shoulder and put her hood over her hair, then covered the baby carefully with the corner of the thick blanket.

"I'll help you out," he offered. "Give me the bag."

"Thanks." She slipped it off and handed it to him, then Joe opened the door to the back porch.

She turned to wave at Peter and Janie. "Bye, kids. Merry Christmas!"

"Merry Christmas!" they called in unison, their mouths stuffed with bacon.

The back door opened just as they reached it, and Hank hurried inside. He was covered with snow, which he stamped off his boots on the mat. He stopped short when he saw Sylvie.

"Hello there," he said, removing his snow-dusted cap.

"Hi," she said, and Joe hurried to explain.

"We had some company, Hank. This is Sylvie. She, uh, got lost. Sylvie, this is Hank Cavendish, the kids' grandfather."

"I thought I saw a strange car," he drawled, his face creasing into a smile when he realized she carried a child. "Where are you and the baby headed, little lady?"

"Back to town."

"Well, unless you have four-wheel drive in that little car of yours, you're not gonna make it."

"Surely it's not that bad yet."

"I just came from town and even in the truck, I was lucky to make it home. You'd best turn around and go back inside. I can't believe Joe was going to let you out of here."

Joe walked past him and opened the door. A strong wind took the door and smacked it against the house before he retrieved it and fastened the latch. Whirling snow stung his face. "What the hell is going on?"

"Kind of a bad one, I hear. We gonna go in where it's warm or stand out here and complain about the weather?"

He winked at Sylvie, who tried to smile, but Joe could see that she looked worried. "I can't stay here."

"Thirty minutes ago you were planning to stay for a lifetime," Joe reminded. He figured he might as well resign himself to having company for one night. He couldn't let her go out in the storm. With his luck, she'd get stuck and he'd end up spending half the night rescuing her.

Hank's mouth gaped open. "You mean it's true?"

"What?"

"You advertised for a wife?"

Oh, hell. He didn't dare look at Sylvie. "How would you know about that?"

"Folks at the Playhouse were asking me about it. Seems you put your ad up in some conspicuous places." He chuckled, and moved past both of them to the kitchen door. "If you wanted to get married, all you had to do was spend a few Saturdays in town. You'd meet women if you ever left the ranch."

"What conspicuous places?"

"You can stand out here and freeze your, uh, toes off, but I'm going inside." He opened the door and sniffed. "Bacon?"

"Come on," Joe said, motioning Sylvie back into the kitchen.

"I can't—"

He was running out of patience. "You can't get back to town. You have to stay here tonight."

He heard the kids' happy cries. "Grandpa!" They screamed, meaning Hank had put his cold hands on the backs of their necks. The old man got a big kick out of teasing them.

Hank reappeared in the doorway. "You two figuring out a wedding day or are you coming inside before these rug rats eat all the food?"

Joe followed Sylvie back into the warmth of

the kitchen. "What conspicuous places?" he repeated.

"The café's front window, for one," Hank said, hooking his wet jacket over the back of a kitchen chair.

Joe turned to the kids. "Where else did you go today?"

Two sets of wide brown eyes faced him. "Lots of places," Peter finally said. "I told her it was a dumb idea, but she wouldn't listen."

"Who?" asked their grandfather.

"Karen."

"Ah." He poured himself a cup of coffee. "I should have guessed."

"It's not funny, Hank." He took his coat and his father-in-law's and hung them on hooks inside the door.

"No," Hank agreed, glancing toward Sylvie with a look of sympathy. "You drove up here to apply for the job, huh?"

"Yes," she replied, uncovering the baby's face.

"Well," the old man said, his expression softening as he saw the child. "You and the little one must be worn-out. Has Joe fed you?"

"No, but—"

"Fix the little gal a plate," he said, putting his mug on the counter. He walked over to Sylvie and held out his arms. "Let me hold the little one for you, honey. Been a long time since I've had the pleasure."

She gave him up without a protest, then

shrugged out of her jacket and draped it behind her on the chair.

"Where's Karen?"

Joe stood at the stove and dumped a healthy portion of eggs and French toast on a plate. "Karen's in her room. She can sleep with Janie tonight, and Sylvie can take her room."

"I can sleep on the couch," the woman said.

"No." He wasn't going to have a strange woman wandering all over the house in her nightclothes.

Hank grinned. "Guess things are going to work out just fine. It's about time we had some female company around here."

Janie nodded. "Karen said we'd get a mom for Christmas."

"She did, did she?"

"Yep." The child licked pancake syrup from her fork. "She's always right."

Peter nodded, anxious to be part of the conversation. "She said Uncle Joe wasn't gonna do it, so somebody had to."

Joe set a plate of food in front of Sylvie and tried not to notice that the tiny woman had one hell of a figure. He backed away from her surprised thanks and figured maybe he should go to town more. Maybe even have a beer at the Playhouse, stay out later than nine o'clock and see what happened. He fixed his own plate and headed back to the table.

"Karen's in trouble," he reminded the children as he sat at his customary spot. "For not minding her own business."

Sylvie turned wide blue eyes in his direction. "She's not going to eat dinner?"

"She can wait awhile," he said, wishing she wouldn't look at him as if he starved children on a regular basis.

"It's not wrong to want a mother," she said.

"It was wrong to advertise for one all over town."

Hank cleared his throat. "Aw, heck, Joe. The kid's only eleven."

"All over town?" Sylvie repeated.

Joe put down his fork. "You might not be the only woman coming up here to marry me, Ms. Smith."

"I didn't see any traffic jams on the way up here, Mr. Brockett."

He didn't mean to find her smile entrancing. "Well," he drawled, "I guess we'll have to wait and see who shows up in the morning."

3

KAREN PULLED A CHAIR over to the window and waited to see the lights of Sylvie's car illuminate the yard. She watched her grandpa's truck bounce up to the side of the garage, saw the snowflakes whirling in the glow of the yard light as he headed toward the house, put her face close to the chilled glass to make certain she wouldn't miss Sylvie's wave.

She would never forgive Uncle Joe for messing this up. Never, ever. Sylvie was perfect mother material, but Uncle Joe wouldn't keep her. Karen couldn't figure out why not. He needed someone to help him cook and clean and take care of them all. That was what a wife did. There would be games to play and cookies to bake and someone to understand when Karen said she needed new jeans.

Karen had given this a lot of thought. She'd made a list. She'd prayed to her mom, who was in heaven and watching over her and Janie and Peter. She'd prayed to her daddy and even to the grandmother she didn't remember, just to make sure that they were all on her side. She figured they'd want her to be happy, and nothing was going to make her happy except getting a mother. She'd made it a Christmas wish so it would sound important.

Uncle Joe was hopeless. Sylvie was beautiful and her baby had the cutest little hands. He'd surprised her when his little fingers had curled around hers, just like he was happy he was going to have a big sister.

Karen wiped the condensation from the window with her sleeve. No Sylvie, no Uncle Joe. Her heart beat a little faster when she heard muffled voices in the kitchen. She tiptoed across her bedroom and opened the door to see if she could hear. Maybe Uncle Joe had changed his mind. Maybe Grandpa would make Uncle Joe keep Sylvie. Maybe Sylvie was afraid of the storm and didn't want to drive her car. Karen crossed the hall to the listening place, where the grate let warm air and voices rise upstairs above the hall. She got on her knees and put her ear against the grate, but she didn't hear Sylvie's voice for a long moment.

"—going to eat dinner?"

Was that Sylvie's voice? Karen dared a smile. Sylvie must be talking about her, since she was the only one not downstairs digging into a plate of bacon and French toast. Her stomach grumbled a little as the smell of bacon wafted upward. Uncle Joe had burned it again.

And Sylvie was still here. She heard the clatter of dishes and silverware.

Karen wished everyone wouldn't talk at once. How was she supposed to understand what they were saying?

"Karen!" Uncle Joe's voice boomed up the stairs. "Come on down and have your supper!"

She wiggled backward and kicked her door so it would make a creaky sound, like she had just opened it. "What?"

"I said, come down and have supper," he replied, louder this time.

"Okay."

Karen scrambled to her feet and hurried to the stairs before he could change his mind. She would have to pretend she was really sorry about putting that ad in the supermarket. She would have to act sad and not smile too much, even though she wanted to giggle and twirl around until she was dizzy. She would eat her supper and help put the dishes in the dishwasher and she would wipe the sticky syrup off the table and say "please" and "thank you" and even "I'm sorry" to everyone.

But in her heart she was the happiest girl in Montana, because Sylvie hadn't left. Because Karen knew her Christmas wish was coming true.

SYLVIE WISHED SHE HADN'T eaten quite so much. Certain that Mr. Brockett thought she must have been close to starvation before arriving at the ranch, she left two bites of French toast on her plate.

"I love snow." Karen beamed at her from across the table.

Sylvie didn't. The storm had inflated an embarrassing incident into an unending predicament involving sleeping in a stranger's house and enduring the odd looks the handsome rancher sent her way. He thought she was crazy. And he had every reason to believe she was.

This hadn't been one of her better days.

Janie, finished with her supper, stood close to her grandfather. "What about the tree?"

"The tree?" He looked at the younger man. Sylvie wondered if they were father and son. They didn't look at all alike, except for the jeans and similar flannel shirts they wore, and the look of men who had worked outdoors for most of their lives. Joe Brockett was tall and lean, with strong features and a hawklike nose. His dark eyes held no hint of warmth or laughter; Sylvie didn't think he was a person who smiled easily or often. Hank, on the other hand, was a short, barrel-chested man who clearly adored his grandchildren and was at ease holding Dillon. He was balding, with silver hair and light gray eyes. Janie resembled him, but dark-haired Peter looked more like he belonged to his Uncle Joe.

"She's talking about the Christmas tree," Joe explained, as if the very word "Christmas" was distasteful.

Brothers, Sylvie decided. Joe must be raising his brother's children, so Hank would have to be the father of the children's mother? She couldn't think too well, considering she'd had a total of six hours of sleep in the past two days.

"Well, well," Hank said. "It's that time of year again?"

Janie and Peter giggled.

"You know it is," the boy said. "Ten—nine days to go before Christmas."

Sylvie put her hand over her mouth to hide a yawn. The warm kitchen was making her sleepy, but she hoped the caffeine would kick in soon. She smiled at the dark-haired boy. "Janie told me what she wanted Santa to bring her. What are *you* hoping for?"

He shrugged, suddenly shy. "I dunno."

"You don't?" his grandfather asked, obviously surprised. "I thought you wanted some kind of *Star Wars* thing."

"Micro Machines," Karen explained. "Those really little things."

Peter nodded and dared a shy glance toward Sylvie. "Yeah."

"What other things do boys like? I'd better know, because Dillon will want them someday."

"*Star Wars* stuff," Peter said. "Action figures, Lego, games, stuff like that." He rose to his knees on the chair and peered at the sleeping baby. "He's not gonna want that stuff now."

"He'll grow," Sylvie assured the boy.

"Doesn't seem possible," Hank said, "but you were little like this not too long ago."

Peter frowned. "I was?"

"Yessir, and you could scream the house down, too, when you were hungry. Your mama had her hands full keeping you quiet."

Joe scraped his chair back and removed his dirty dishes. "Karen, you clear the table and load the dishwasher."

"Okay."

Sylvie stood, too. "Let me help," she said.

"No." He didn't smile—not that she expected him to.

"Why not?"

"You're company," Karen explained over the clatter of piling silverware on top of plates.

"Not exactly." Sylvie began to pick up dirty dishes. "I can clear the table. If I don't move around I'm going to fall asleep."

"You'll be sleeping in Karen's room," Joe said. "You have stuff out in the car you need?"

"A couple of suitcases," she said. "And Dillon's car seat and little bed."

"I'll get them." He reached for his jacket as the phone rang, so he grabbed that instead. "Hello?" Joe's gaze landed on Hank. "Yeah, sure. He's right here." He held out the receiver. "Hank. For you."

The older man took the phone without disturbing the baby in his arms. "Hello?" He paused. "Oh, yeah. No, it wasn't too bad." Another pause. "Oh, that? Turns out the kids did it." Pause. "Okay, I'll tell him. Yeah. Sure." Pause. "Bye."

He hung up the phone and returned to his chair.

"Who was that?" Joe hesitated by the back door.

"Ruby. You know Ruby. She has that beauty parlor on Main Street by the corner of—"

"I know where it is," Joe said, looking as if he was trying not to smile. "What'd she want?"

Sylvie continued to clear the table, but she was surprised to see the man's discomfort. "She just wanted to know if I made it home okay."

Joe jammed his hat on his head. "Nice of her."

"Yeah."

"So you were partying at the Playhouse with Ruby, huh?"

"Not exactly. She'd seen the ad at the diner and she thought it was me looking for a wife."

"Did she want the job?"

The kids giggled, which Hank didn't seem to mind. He winked at Peter. "Well, she might've been interested."

"I'm going into town tomorrow and taking those damn signs down," Joe muttered. "I'll be the laughingstock of the county by Monday."

"Oh, there's no hurry," Hank assured him. "Folks are already laughing. Another day or two won't make any difference."

Joe eyed his older niece. "If you ever pull anything like this again, you'll be grounded until you're eighteen and ready to go off to college. You got that?"

"We just wanted a mother like everyone else."

"Bedtime," Joe said, motioning to the other two after Karen stormed upstairs. He didn't wait to see if they obeyed before he left the house.

"Sorry about all this. My daughter, the kids' mother, died three years ago," Hank explained, setting Dillon in Sylvie's arms. "I'd better go up and tuck them in."

"And their father?" She couldn't help asking.

"Joe's brother. He was in the car with her. It was one week before Christmas," Hank said. "This is a hard time of year."

"I'm sorry."

He sighed. "Well, it sure ain't been easy, but we've done our best."

"They're nice children."

"Yeah, but they want something Joe and I can't give them," he said, then left the room. She heard his footsteps on the stairs as she sat in the suddenly quiet room. Sylvie didn't want to care. She really didn't. She didn't want to feel sorry for the children or the men taking care of them. She wanted to drive away with Dillon and get on with her life, but the snowstorm prevented her from going anywhere.

But upstairs a little girl missed her mother, so Sylvie couldn't sit there and do nothing. She adjusted Dillon's weight in her arms, then headed for the stairs. Surely she could talk to Karen and make her feel better. At least she could try.

Tomorrow, Sylvie decided. Tomorrow she would get on with her life.

"SURE WAS A STRANGE DAY," Hank said, coming up behind Joe in the barn.

"Yeah. In more ways than one." Joe finished tossing hay to the horses and turned around to glance out the window. He couldn't see a damn thing except snow. "This is one hell of a storm."

"You've heard of the Blizzard of '48?"

"Yeah."

"Fifty years ago," Hank said, "almost to the day. They had to airlift food out to the ranches. There was no way anyone could get out."

"You think it's going to be that bad?"

He shrugged. "I dunno. I don't have a good feeling, though."

They listened as the wind whipped around the old barn.

"Sounds bad."

"We've had worse."

"Maybe," the older man admitted. "In '48."

"I'm done." Joe wanted nothing more than to finish up work and grab a hot shower before bed. "Did you get the woman settled?"

"Sure did. She and that baby of hers are all set. Karen made up her bed and got some extra blankets. I sure hope we don't lose electricity."

"We probably will," Joe said, hooking the handle of the pitchfork on the wall. "The wind's getting worse."

"You done?"

"Yeah. I'm going in."

"Don't be too mad at the kids," Hank said when Joe paused at the door. "Their mom's been gone three years now."

"Hard to believe."

"Karen looks just like her."

"Yeah." He shook his head. "Crazy kid. I can't believe she thought she'd find a wife for me at Buttrey's."

Hank chuckled. "There's a woman on the Rocky T tonight, so it worked, didn't it?"

Joe remembered the scared expression on Sylvie's face when she talked about applying for the job at the ranch. "Why would a woman want to marry a stranger? I just don't get it."

"Well, women think different than we do."

"No kidding."

"Maybe she's just hit rock bottom."

Joe chuckled. "Meaning 'rock bottom' is marrying me."

"You should have married a long time ago."

"I never wanted to." He changed the subject so that he wouldn't have to lie to his best friend again. "Where's that baby's father? What kind of man deserts a woman and a child?"

"That's none of our business, Joe." Hank opened the barn door and peered outside. "Maybe she ran away. Maybe the bastard beat her. Maybe she never told him she was gonna have a baby. Maybe he's dead. Hell, there are all sorts of things that go on while you and I are feedin' cattle and worryin' about the weather."

"She'll be gone tomorrow," Joe said, needing to reassure himself.

"Maybe," Hank drawled. "But if this storm keeps up, you could have company for more than just a night."

"Hell."

Hank hesitated before leaving the barn. "What's bothering you, son?"

He pulled the collar of his jacket up high against his neck. "I don't think she's got much sense, that's all. A woman ought to know better than to go offering herself to strangers."

"She's a pretty little gal."

"I don't see what that has to do with anything."

Hank shrugged. "Just thinking out loud, that's all. Maybe the kids are right."

"You've lost your mind, too."

"No, hear me out. Maybe it's time we hired a housekeeper. A woman. You know, to take care of the house and do the cooking and all that."

"We talked about that before, Hank. We couldn't afford it."

"We can now, I'll bet. Especially if we offered room and board. Why, I'll bet someone would be glad to have a job like this."

"Thirty miles out of town?"

"Why not? We could put up an ad, like Karen did, and just see if anyone turns up for the job."

"Now I see where Karen gets her ideas."

"Then again," Hank said, ignoring Joe's comment, "we've already got someone willing to take the job."

"We don't have a job."

"Sylvie was willing to be a wife. I'll bet she'd jump at the chance to be a housekeeper. With three squares a day and a roof over her head, she and that boy of hers would be in hog heaven."

"No."

"You should think about it."

"No." He didn't know how he could make it any clearer than that, but Hank didn't seem to hear him.

"While you're thinking, I'm going home to watch the weather channel and see what's happening. If I hear anything important I'll let you know."

"Can you see to make it back?"

"I left some lights on."

"I'll walk part of the way with you," Joe said, switching off the indoor light as he followed Hank out into the storm. He made sure the door was latched securely.

"You're finished out here?"

"Yeah." He was finished with the whole damn day. A strange woman, a storm, a screeching baby, and three kids who expected him to jump up and down with happiness at the thought of Christmas had just about worn him out. He and Hank hunched against the wind and trudged toward Hank's two-bedroom cabin. Joe could have walked it blindfolded; he'd lived in that cabin during his brother's marriage before moving back to the main house after the accident.

"Want a drink?" Hank called over the wind.

Joe shook his head and didn't follow Hank up the porch steps. He lifted his hand in farewell, then turned toward his own house. He could barely see the porch light through the swirling snow, but it was enough to guide him home.

The strange day was real close to being over, and it had been one he wouldn't want to live over again. He didn't need a wife, and he sure didn't need a housekeeper. And if he decided he did need one, she wouldn't be a homeless stranger with an infant. No, he needed Christmas to come and go with as little fuss as possible. Then everything would get back to normal.

MORNING COULDN'T COME soon enough. Oh, the bed was snug enough and the small bedroom, cluttered with horse posters and books, was warm, but throughout the night Sylvie had worried that Dillon's cries would wake the children. She'd been afraid she would sleep so soundly that she wouldn't hear him right away.

Every three hours he would waken, but Sylvie heard no sounds from the rest of the house during those times. Even now, with dim morning light coming through the shades, Sylvie couldn't tell if anyone else was awake. Even Dillon had nursed sleepily and returned uncomplaining to his bed. Sylvie tiptoed around the room and packed up their belongings. She'd slept enough to feel rested—or as close to rested as a new mother could feel—and told herself she looked forward to leaving this place. She'd peered through the window, but the glass was frosted over and prevented her from seeing how deep the snow was. The wind still gusted against the house, but that didn't mean the storm continued. She dressed in jeans and a clean sweatshirt, used the white-tiled bathroom that connected Karen's bedroom with Janie's, and brushed her hair back into a soft ponytail at the nape of her neck.

She would leave right after breakfast—or even before, if the children were awake. She wouldn't leave without saying goodbye and thanking them for their hospitality.

But that wasn't going to be so easy, Sylvie realized when she left Dillon sleeping and tiptoed downstairs. She could smell fresh coffee and there was a light on in the kitchen. Mr. Brockett sat at the table, an open account ledger at his elbow. A small television, tucked underneath a set of cupboards, was tuned in to the weather channel.

"Good morning," he said, looking up as she hesitated in the doorway, so it was too late to tiptoe back upstairs unnoticed.

"Good morning."

"Help yourself to coffee," he said, still not smiling. "I hope you like it strong."

"Thank you." She didn't want to sit at the table and make small talk with this quiet man, but to return upstairs now would seem rude.

"The cups are in the cupboard above the coffeepot."

"Oh." She went over to the counter, found a thick blue mug and filled it with coffee. Instead of sitting down at the table, she went over to the window and looked outside—then wished she hadn't.

"We're in the middle of a blizzard," he said. "We're lucky we still have power, but it could go out anytime."

She wouldn't be leaving this morning, that much was clear. Even if she got the car uncovered, she'd never make it out of the drive to the county road. "It hasn't stopped snowing at all, has it?"

"And won't anytime soon, according to the weather reports." He motioned toward the television. "See for yourself."

She sat down in a chair closest to the TV and, sipping the coffee, watched for a few minutes. Mr. Brockett got up and refilled his cup, then came over to watch with her. "You're lucky you weren't on the road last night," he said. "You would have been driving right into it."

"How long is it supposed to snow?" She wanted to go home more than she'd thought possible. This trip had gone from one disaster to another.

"Another day, maybe two. I've been outside. There are six-foot drifts between here and the barn."

"What about the animals? Will they be all right?"

"I've fed those I could," he said, walking over to the window. He frowned. "As soon as it gets lighter, Hank and I will ride out and see about the rest. I'm hoping that they found shelter in the hollows." Joe turned away from the window and set his cup down on the table. "I guess I'd better go shovel some more," he said, lifting his coat from its hook by the door. "Help yourself to breakfast. You should find everything you need in the fridge."

"Is there anything I can do to help?"

"If the kids wake up before I get back, tell

them where I am," he said. "And don't let them go outside."

"I won't," she promised, watching him wrap a long wool scarf around his face and neck until only his eyes were visible. He pulled on thick leather gloves and went onto the back porch, where she heard him stomp his feet into boots. She didn't envy him his job this morning.

And she owed him a favor. Sylvie opened the refrigerator, then assessed the contents of the cupboards. She would make the rancher a breakfast fit for a king. After he tasted her cinnamon rolls, the man might even be sorry he'd said he didn't want a wife.

Sylvie laughed to herself, thinking how ridiculous it was for her to have answered that ad yesterday. For a few brief hours she'd thought she'd hit rock bottom, but today was a new day. She was rested, Dillon was asleep, there was a can of yeast in the refrigerator just waiting to be opened and, for this morning, she could pretend this cozy kitchen was hers.

4

HANK FIGURED HIS BEST ideas came to him after a good night's sleep. And this particular idea was a real doozy. He drank his coffee and fried up a couple of eggs, toasted wheat bread and opened a new jar of apple butter to spread liberally on his toast, but all the while he was congratulating himself on how darn smart he was.

A man didn't live sixty-five years without learning a few things.

Joe's knock at the door was no surprise; there would be plenty to do today in order to make sure the cattle were safe, but he was used to storms. He hollered at Joe to come inside, heard him stomping the snow off his boots before the unlocked door swung open.

"Mornin'," Hank said, going back to spreading apple butter on his toast. "You want breakfast?"

"I ate already, thanks." The younger man stepped carefully onto the old rug placed in front of the door. He unwound his scarf and cursed as snow showered the rug.

"Sit," Hank said. "Don't worry about your boots. A little snow isn't gonna hurt this old floor."

Joe unzipped his jacket, but didn't remove it. "I just came to see if you wanted to ride with me over to the winter pasture to check the cattle there. I'm hoping they'll drift in. I found about a hundred of the yearlings behind the long shed, so they're okay for now."

"Yeah, I'll go. You're gonna need help, especially if you've gotta shovel out some drifts."

"I already cleared a path by the barn, but I don't know how long it will be before it blows back again."

"Hell of a storm," Hank said, taking a bite of toast. "Pour yourself some coffee and sit down. Let me finish my breakfast and then we'll go see how bad it is."

Joe sat. "I've had enough coffee."

Hank thought he should test the waters, so to speak. "Everyone still sleeping up there at the house?"

"The woman was up," he said, frowning as if he didn't like the idea of having her around. Hank hid a smile and looked at his plate. "She thought she'd be leaving this morning."

"Guess she hadn't looked out the window."

"Guess not." Joe sat down at the table and fidgeted with the saltshaker. "She's looking out for the kids while we're outside."

"Well, now. That's a help."

"Don't start up, Hank," Joe said, pushing the saltshaker out of reach.

Hank widened his eyes. "I just said that was a help, that's all. Wasn't exactly a lie, neither."

"We don't need help."

"That's your opinion," he muttered, finishing the last of his eggs.

"Jeez, Hank," Joe sputtered. "You want a woman up here so badly, why don't you find one for yourself?"

Hank pretended to consider the suggestion, then shook his head. "Naw. I was married thirty-two years to the best woman in Montana. I might just be too old to start looking around again, but you're young. You need the... company."

Joe stood and zipped his jacket. "I *need* to get outside and start feeding cattle before they freeze to death. You coming with me or are you going to sit there and give advice all morning?"

"I might."

"Well, don't waste your breath. The last thing we need around here is a woman like that."

Hank chuckled as he pushed his plate aside. For the first time in three years, he began to look forward to Christmas.

AT FIRST HE FIGURED he was hallucinating. Joe could swear he smelled fresh bread baking when Janie opened the kitchen door to greet him. He removed his snow-covered jacket and boots and left them on the back porch. Later he would build a fire in the woodstove and hang them to dry, but now he was hungry and cold after four hours chasing cows and fighting the north wind.

"Uncle Joe!" Janie cried, jumping up and down with excitement.

"Hey, kid." He found a pair of old leather moccasins and slipped them on as Hank entered the porch from outside.

"Sylvie's still here!" the child announced. "Hi, Grandpa!"

"I know." Joe ruffled her hair as he stepped through the doorway into the kitchen. He definitely smelled bread and his stomach growled in appreciation of the best odor known to man. "We came in to get warm. What smells so good?"

The sight that greeted him stopped him in his tracks. He heard Hank behind him talking to Janie, but Joe stared at the woman at the kitchen counter. She looked prettier than he remembered, or maybe that was because her cheeks were flushed and she was laughing at something Peter was telling her. The boy stood on a chair at the counter and stuck his fingers into a mixing bowl.

Karen turned from the sink. "Uncle Joe, do you see what Sylvie made?"

He found his voice and took another step closer to the counter. "No, but I smell something good."

"Cinnamon rolls," Sylvie said. "I hope you like them."

"How'd you do that?"

"You had all the ingredients," she explained. "I hope you don't mind."

No man in his right mind would mind a woman baking cinnamon rolls. "Of course not," was all he could say, eyeing the pan of rolls on the counter.

"I'm making frosting," Peter announced, showing him the bowl.

"Go ahead and drizzle it on the rolls," Sylvie told him, helping him with the spoon. "And then we'll serve some to your uncle and grandfather."

"Oh, boy." Peter grinned and wiggled a stream of white frosting over the pans. "It's like paint, huh?"

"Yes, just keep it inside the pan."

"Aren't we the lucky men," Hank said, rubbing his hands together. "I'm sure glad we didn't get lost in the storm and miss out on all this good food."

Janie hugged him. "You got lost?"

"No, honey, Grandpa was just teasing," he assured her, swinging her into his arms. "It's cold out there, though."

"Did the cows die?"

"No," her grandfather said. "I think we found most of them in time."

Joe didn't know what to do with himself, so he went over to the kitchen table and sat down. The baby, snug in his portable car seat, slept in the middle of the table. If Joe hadn't seen the infant's eyelids flutter a couple of times, he would have figured the baby was unconscious. "Are you sure he doesn't mind all this noise?"

Sylvie shook her head. "I think the voices put him to sleep. He liked looking at the kids, too."

"He smiled at me," Karen said, placing a cup

of hot coffee in front of Joe. "I'll be right back with yours, Grandpa."

Hank sat down and Janie crawled into his lap. "Well, now, this is service."

"Sylvie used to cook in a restaurant," Karen told him, returning with another cup of coffee.

"She did?" Hank bent to take a sip. "Don't wriggle, Janie. Grandpa doesn't want to spill coffee on you."

Joe watched as Sylvie cut the rolls and put them on plates. She seemed to know what she was doing, all right. "Where did you work, Sylvie?"

"Oh, in lots of places," she said, taking a cloth and wiping the frosting from Peter's sticky fingers. "I made an omelet. Are you hungry?"

"Yes, but you didn't have to go to all this work."

She smiled again, and he wished she wouldn't. He didn't like the way his chest got all tight. He didn't want to be attracted to her. Hell, he didn't even want to *like* her.

"It's not much work. And besides, I wanted to repay your hospitality, Mr. Brockett. A meal seems like a small enough thing to do."

"Call me Joe. And you don't owe me anything." It was the other way around, after what those kids had put her through.

She looked away and lifted a skillet off the stove. "I fed the children, but I made another one for you and Hank."

"I am hungry," Joe admitted, but he felt a little awkward being waited on. Sylvie Smith was a stranger, and yet she seemed as if she belonged in his kitchen. No, not his kitchen. Deb's kitchen. He watched as Sylvie prepared the plates of food and brought them over to the table. She set one in front of each man and, as she leaned near him, Joe inhaled the strangely erotic scent of cinnamon.

Janie squirmed off Hank's lap and climbed onto her own chair to look at the sleeping baby. Karen and Peter gathered around the table to watch Joe and Hank sample the cinnamon rolls as Sylvie poured herself a cup of coffee and returned to the table to take a seat.

"Good, huh?" Peter asked.

"Very good," Joe managed to say after swallowing. He'd never tasted anything so delicious in his life.

"The best I've ever had," Hank added, and Joe watched Sylvie smile with delight. "In fact," he continued, "I was thinking—"

"Hank," Joe interrupted. "How long did you say this storm was going to last?"

"It should quit sometime late this afternoon," Hank answered, frowning at Joe. "Least that's what the weatherman said."

Sylvie turned anxious blue eyes on Joe. "Do you think I'll be able to drive to town after the snow stops?"

"Well, I can—"

"Drifts," Hank declared. "There'll be lots of drifts between here and town, and you and the boy don't want to drive into one. Why, back in

'48, people died driving into drifts. They plumb froze to death."

"They did? How awful!"

"Wow!" Peter breathed.

Hank nodded and looked grim. "You've got at least thirty miles between here and town, Sylvie. That's a lot of drifting snow between you and safety."

"But won't they plow the roads?"

Joe figured this had gone far enough. "Of course they will, soon as it stops snowing and maybe before that. The kind of storm that Hank's talking about happens about once every hundred years."

She still looked worried.

"I can follow you to town," Joe offered. "To make sure you get there safely."

"What happens if you *both* get stuck?" Hank protested. "What'll you do then?"

"That's true," Sylvie agreed. "It's not right to risk your life, too."

Joe gave the old man a withering look, but Hank ignored him. "No one's risking anything. Later on I'll plow the road—the one on the ranch—and then we'll see what the main road is like."

Hank finished his cinnamon roll and smiled as if he'd tasted a chunk of heaven. "I have a better idea."

There would be no stopping him, Joe realized. Hank was determined to offer this woman a job, but Joe wasn't going to let him do it with three little allies cheering him on and getting their hopes up. They'd think they'd gotten away with something, no doubt. "Wait a minute," Joe said, turning to look at the kids. "Go watch television or something for a while."

Karen stared at him. "Why?"

"What do you mean, *why*? Just go watch TV while the grown-ups talk."

"I get left out of everything," Karen grumbled. "I never get to hear anything good."

"Go on," Joe said, trying not to smile.

"We'll go upstairs and play cards," the girl declared. After some sputtering by the younger children, the three kids left the room. Joe heard them giggling as they ran up the stairs.

"Why don't you have another roll, Hank?"

"In a minute."

Sylvie stood. "Let me get you some more coffee."

Hank held out his cup. "I guess that's an offer I can't rightly refuse."

"Sit down," Joe told her. "You don't have to wait on us." He brought the pot of coffee to the table and refilled the three cups, then set the empty carafe on the counter. "We're used to taking care of ourselves," he explained.

Sylvie chuckled. "I guess my waitress habits are showing."

"I thought you were a cook."

"That, too," she said.

Hank cleared his throat. "I had myself an idea this morning."

Joe leaned back in his chair. There would be

no stopping the old man now, and if he tried he would appear rude.

"We need someone here to help with the kids and do the cooking and all that woman stuff," Hank continued. "I'm getting too old to keep up with those kids now and Joe's got his hands full running this ranch."

"Your granddaughter advertised for a wife," Sylvie said. "It sounds like that's exactly what the two of you need."

Hank chuckled, but Joe still didn't see anything funny about what Karen had done. "Neither one of us is getting married anytime soon," Hank assured her. "But we could use some help around here, especially now that it's Christmas. Are you looking for a job?"

She would refuse, Joe thought as he saw the embarrassed expression cross Sylvie's face. Which would be for the best, he reminded himself. He didn't need this pretty woman pouring him coffee and serving him homemade bread and smiling at him. He was a man who was used to being alone, used to his own bachelor ways. And he liked it that way.

"Yes," the damn woman told Hank. "I'm looking for a job."

Joe's heart sank. He stared across the table at Hank, but the old man ignored his glare.

"You free for the holidays?" Hank asked.

Sylvie glanced toward her sleeping baby, then back at Hank. "We haven't made any plans."

"You're not going somewhere special for Christmas?"

"No." Her chin lifted, telling Joe that the old man had hit a sore spot. So the little lady didn't have any family that she wanted to visit.

"Well, then," his father-in-law drawled, "why don't you work here?"

"For the holidays?" she asked.

"For as long as you want."

"I suppose I could, for the holidays," she agreed, and turned to look at Joe. "Mr. Brockett, what do you think about all of this?"

He opened his mouth but couldn't think of a damn thing to say except, "Could I have another roll?"

Later, after Hank and Sylvie had discussed the details and he had eaten two more cinnamon buns, Joe knew he should have spoken up. He should have asked about her background and what she was doing on the road with an infant. She could be insane. She could be a criminal. And he and Hank could be convicted of harboring her.

Joe rubbed his forehead. He'd had too much coffee. Anyone with eyes could see that Sylvie Smith couldn't hurt anyone. Look how badly she'd felt about Karen when the kid had locked herself in her room. And she treated that baby of hers so gently, as if the sun rose and set on him. The way Deb had treated her babies, actually. Joe sat alone in the kitchen and knew he should do something about Sylvie, but he didn't know what. The family had already decided to keep her, and nothing he said would make any difference.

Still, it seemed like a man ought to make an effort to know who the hell was sleeping under his roof.

"BUT YOU PROMISED," Karen said, her hands on her hips. "You said we'd get it today."

"Has anyone looked out the window lately?" The rancher pointed to the bank of windows across from the sofa, as if none of them knew what windows were.

"The children know it's snowing, Mr. Brockett," Sylvie replied, wondering if the man was always this grumpy. "They're excited about getting the tree, that's all." And she was excited, too. About Christmas. About her new job. About giving Dillon a temporary family for the holidays. If Mr. Brockett would only lighten up, everything would be perfect. He hadn't complained about her cooking, hadn't said a word of opposition to Hank's offer of a job, hadn't seemed to mind when she'd fixed the children's lunch and cleaned up the kitchen.

The irritating man ran one large hand through his hair and frowned. "I'm not taking kids outside to hunt a tree in weather like this. Tomorrow," he said, "after school will be soon enough."

"If there *is* school," Karen added, flopping into a chair.

"Well, then, as soon as the storm is over. Even if I have to buy a tree in town," he promised.

"*Buy* a tree?" Peter gasped. "We've gotta cut

it down, and Grandpa always lets me hold the saw."

"If we can't get to the woods," his uncle said, "we'll have no choice but to buy one."

Sylvie figured it was time to change the subject and have some questions answered about her duties. "Do you take a bus to school?"

Karen answered. "Yep. It picks us up at seven fifty-three."

"'Us'?" Sylvie tucked Dillon into his car seat propped in the corner of the couch and watched as his eyes closed and his breathing slowed.

"All of us. Pete goes to kindergarten, then to play group where Janie is."

"What's play group?"

Joe, still looking out the window, answered the question. "It's with Janie's preschool, and the kids come home on the bus with the elementary-school kids. I usually go to town to pick Janie up at noon, but sometimes she stays all day."

Janie sighed. "You hafta be five." She climbed onto the couch and snuggled against Sylvie's side. "I want a tree."

"It's too cold and windy outside," Sylvie told her. "Your Uncle Joe will get a Christmas tree as soon as the snow stops."

"Yeah," he said, "maybe tomorrow."

Sylvie felt sorry for the child who sighed against her shoulder. "You don't need a tree to decorate the house."

Karen turned away from the window. "You don't?"

"Of course not. You have Christmas decorations, don't you?"

"Up in the attic."

"Well, there you go," Sylvie declared, wanting the kids to look happy again. "We'll get them from the attic and see what we can use. We'll decorate the house instead and then, whenever your tree comes, you can decorate that, too."

Joe finally moved away from the window. "You'll need a ladder."

"If you tell me where one is, I'd be glad to get it."

"I'll take care of it," he answered. "I don't want the kids getting hurt messing around with that stuff."

"All right." He could do anything he wanted. It was his house, after all. She wondered why he didn't seem happy about Christmas.

But that was no reason to take it out on the children.

Joe Brockett hesitated in the doorway of the living room. The look he gave Sylvie was anything but pleased. "I hope you know what you're getting into. That stuff up there is a mess."

"I'll take care of it. Isn't that what I was hired for?" It didn't hurt to remind him that she was doing her job.

"Hired?" Karen perked up. "You're staying here with us?"

"Until after Christmas," Sylvie replied. "Your

grandfather asked if I would work here until then.''

Peter frowned. ''What's your job?''

''Taking care of the three of you.''

Janie wrapped her arms around Sylvie's neck and planted a wet kiss on her cheek. ''I like you!''

''I like you, too,'' Sylvie managed to say, even though tears stung her eyes. She shouldn't be this moved by the child's affection, she told herself. But then again, it had been a long time since anyone had hugged her. No, she wasn't going to feel sorry for herself. She wasn't going to think about the past. She was going to live in the present for the next nine days until Christmas. It would be like a vacation.

And she wouldn't let the children's uncle hurt their feelings or ruin their Christmas.

''Sylvie,'' the man called, sticking his head into the living room just when she'd thought he'd left. ''Could I have a word with you?''

She checked to make sure Dillon was asleep. ''Karen, will you sit here with him?''

''Sure,'' the girl said, her eyes wide. ''Are you in trouble?''

Sylvie winked. She had only worked here for a few hours, so she didn't see how she could have antagonized the rancher so soon. ''I don't think so.''

Karen didn't look convinced, but she sat down on the couch beside Dillon as Sylvie headed to the hall. Joe Brockett motioned for her to follow him into a small room that was obviously used as an office. An old wooden desk was piled high with papers and ledgers, there were dust-covered issues of *Cattleman's Journal* piled in corners, and the window was protected by a crooked, checkered curtain faded from the sun.

"Have a seat." He perched on the edge of the desk and indicated an armless wooden chair.

She sat where directed and waited for him to continue.

"Who are you?" came the blunt question.

Sylvie straightened. "Sylvia Smith."

"That's your real name?"

"That's as real as it gets," she answered, wishing she had never seen that damn ad. No, she reminded herself. She and Dillon were safe and warm and well fed. There were worse things than answering an ad.

The rancher didn't look convinced. "Lady, the rest of the family might be willing to let a stranger in here without so much as the blink of an eyelash, but not me. Now, who are you and what are you doing in this part of the county?"

"I know it looks a little odd," she said, gripping her hands together in her lap.

"'A little'?"

"Well, I really don't think it's any of your business." There. She'd said it. Joe Brockett would have to back off.

"Think again," he said, not taking his gaze from her face. "The minute you walked in here thinking you were going to be my wife, you became my business."

"I really didn't want to get married, but I was desperate."

His lips tightened. "Thank you."

"You know what I mean. I really wasn't looking for a husband." Well, that wasn't true. She'd had high hopes for finding Billy Ray and living happily ever after. She'd wanted a family, she'd wanted a home, and she'd hoped for a happy reunion. "Not exactly," she added.

"And that baby's father?"

"Isn't around right now."

Joe frowned. "So what are you running away from?"

"Nothing. I was looking for something I couldn't find. Could we leave it at that?"

"For the moment. Are the police after you?"

She almost laughed, but she realized he was serious. "No."

"I can check—and I will—with the county sheriff."

"You go right ahead. My purse is upstairs. You'll find my driver's license in my wallet. Feel free to call the sheriff, the state police, the FBI, whoever you want. I don't have anything to hide, Mr. Brockett."

"Oh?" His eyebrows rose, and the look he gave her was anything but trusting. "Somehow I don't believe that for a minute, Miss Smith."

"It's the truth." She stood. "If you're done asking me questions, I'd like to get back to the children. We have a lot to do before we're ready for Christmas."

5

"YOU LOOK LIKE YOU LOST your best friend," Hank muttered, closing the back door behind him.

"I didn't hear you come in." Joe pushed his untouched mug of coffee aside. He was tired of coffee and tired of this damn storm.

Hank rubbed his hands together to warm them. "I left my wet boots on the porch. I need to shovel it soon. I could barely open the door."

"I'll do it again as soon as the wind stops."

Hank's eyebrows rose as he looked at Joe. "Wind might not stop till June." He poured himself a cup of coffee and looked over the counter. "Any more of those cinnamon buns lying around?"

"You ate them all."

"Where is everyone?

"Can't you hear?"

Hank cocked his head. "'Jingle Bells'?"

"Yeah. I think it's the fifteenth time. Karen found all those old Christmas albums and they've been on the stereo ever since. I got a bunch of stuff down from the attic and put it in the hall, so they've been busy going through it." He looked at his friend, who edged closer to the door as if he couldn't wait to join the celebration. "You shouldn't have done this, Hank. You had no right."

"No right?" Hank echoed. "They're my grandchildren. They deserve to be happy, especially now. And if it makes me happy to give them what they want for Christmas, what's the harm?" With that, he left the room, and Joe could swear he heard the old traitor humming along with the music.

Hank must be getting senile already, having hired a "Christmas woman"—a woman who would stay and take care of the kids.

Blizzards were easier to deal with than women, Joe figured. At least with a blizzard you knew that it would be over and, if you were smart and didn't take any foolish chances, you'd be alive when the snow ended. Women were trickier. There was no end to them; and no matter what a guy did, he sure felt like he'd fallen face first into a seven-foot drift.

It was easy to hate December. Easy to resent every bit of holiday cheer. Easy to wish Sylvie Smith to the devil, or at least to a motel in Willum.

To be fair—and Joe prided himself on being fair—it was more than a little easy to resent a woman—to be fair, any woman—who was in Deb's house, hugging Deb's children, touching Deb's Christmas ornaments. She looked nothing like Deb, of course. So that should have made it easier.

If anything could be called "easy."

Deb—she hated to be called Debbie by anyone but her father—had been tall, with long legs and thick brown hair and green eyes that sparkled with laughter and mischief. This Smith woman was small-boned and delicate, with silky pale yellow hair and blue eyes that held secrets and sadness. But when she smiled, you could swear she'd melt the snow that had drifted against the back-porch door—the same drift he'd shoveled three times already.

He wished she wouldn't smile.

"I MADE IT LAST YEAR." Karen held up a patchwork ornament shaped like a wreath. "It's pretty, huh?"

"Very pretty." Sylvie took the ornament and made certain she admired it properly before handing it back. "You can put the tree ornaments in that empty box for now. "

Janie hugged a stuffed reindeer and peered out the window. "It's still snowing."

"Not as hard," her brother declared, sounding exactly like his uncle.

"Well, good." Sylvie lifted a tangled rope of silver tinsel. She loved all this. It was the stuff of which dreams were made: laughing children and treasured family decorations, Christmas carols on the stereo and snow falling outdoors. All of it was wonderful and worth putting up with Joe Brockett's frown whenever he looked into the living room.

He'd be handsome if he smiled.

"Maybe that means we can get the tree tomorrow."

Karen frowned. "Monday's a school night."

"What time do you go to bed?" Sylvie asked.

"Eight."

"If we had supper early, there would be plenty of time. Do you usually have a lot of homework?"

Karen brightened. "Sometimes, but I can do it fast unless it's math."

"Okay. I'll ask your uncle if he can take you to cut down a tree tomorrow afternoon." She'd rather ask the devil for a bowl of ice cream, but if these children wanted their tree tomorrow, then that's what they would get. Sylvie lifted a tangled strand of lights from the bottom of the cardboard box and held them up. "Who wants to help me get the knots out?"

"I will," Hank said, appearing in the doorway of the living room. He wore thick gray socks and held a cup of coffee in his right hand. "Untangling the lights has always been my job." He winked as he sat down on a free spot on the couch and put his mug on the table beside him. "It's been a long time since I've had a pretty lady to help me, though."

Sylvie smiled her acknowledgment of the compliment, though she knew she looked like a worn-out hag. "Should we wait for the tree?"

"Naw," he said, taking the strand of lights from her hands. "It'll go faster tomorrow if the lights are all set. We can wind them up again real neat, so there won't be any knots tomorrow night."

"That's a good idea." She lifted another set of lights from the box. "I think that's all of them."

He looked over the assortment of cardboard boxes and the array of holiday decorations spread out on the floor and chairs. "There should be more than this," he said, then raised his voice. "Joe! Hey, Joe!"

A moment later the rancher stood at the living-room door. He didn't look happy about being interrupted. "What?"

"We're missing some boxes. Did you get everything out of the attic?"

Joe shrugged. "I got what I could see."

"Well, look again, will you? I don't see Deb's wreath—you know, the calico one." Hank turned to his grandson. "Come here, Pete, and hold on to this end of the cord while I get this knot out."

Unlike his uncle, the little boy looked pleased by Hank's command and hurried over to help. "Okay."

"You'll need to give me a hand," Joe said, not stepping any farther into the room.

"Go with him, Sylvie," Hank said. "You can hold the flashlight."

Joe frowned. "I need you to take the boxes from me, Hank."

"I can do that." Sylvie climbed to her feet and stepped carefully over the decorations.

"I don't think—"

"Aw, Joe," Hank interrupted, not looking at him, "I've got my hands full, here."

Sylvie followed Joe into the hallway. "I'm perfectly capable of holding a flashlight, Mr. Brockett."

"Right." He gestured for her to lead the way up the stairs.

"And I can carry boxes, too," she thought she needed to add, just so he would get the message. "I'm sure this is part of my job."

"Yeah, well," he grumbled, "I didn't hire you, remember?"

She was really getting tired of his attitude. Sylvie stopped and turned around to face him. Even standing two steps higher than the man, she had to look up to look him in the eye. "*Yeah, well*," she said, consciously imitating him as her voice shook, "get over it, will you?"

He glared at her, so she shook the flashlight in his nose. "You may think this a lot of trouble to go through, but I'm trying to do what I was hired to do, which is to give your kids a nice Christmas. You can stomp around here like the Grinch Who Stole Christmas if you want to, but you can *stop* taking your bad moods out on me, you hear?"

"Like the *what?*"

"Grinch. Dr. Seuss. Cartoon."

"Stop waving that flashlight around so close to my nose."

She lowered her hand. "Are you deliberately trying to ruin Christmas?"

"I'm not ruining anything."

"Then it wouldn't hurt you to smile once in a while, show a little holiday spirit."

"And how exactly would you suggest I do that?"

"Stretch your lips in an upward position."

He looked as if he wanted to throttle her, which pleased Sylvie enormously. "I meant the 'holiday spirit' part of your suggestion."

"Just act like you're having a good time. It hurts the children's feelings when you don't join in."

"There's a blizzard—"

"You could sing with us."

"And there are animals that need—"

"Decorating," she declared. "To make the house look festive."

He glared down at her. "Anything else, your highness?"

"Stop making faces at me." She wanted to cry again, which meant her hormones had taken a sudden dive. Or she'd had too much coffee. Or she needed a nap like the one Dillon was enjoying.

"Then stop looking like I'm some kind of monster."

"Are you fighting?" came a small voice from the bottom of the stairs. Sylvie glanced past Joe's shoulder as he turned to look at his younger niece.

Sylvie decided to let Janie's uncle answer that question.

"No," Joe declared. "We're having a discussion."

The little girl's bottom lip quivered. "You're making my ears hurt."

"Go tell Grandpa we'll be back real soon," Joe said, his voice soft. "And see if you can find a song called 'The Little Drummer Boy.' That's my favorite."

Janie brightened. "Okay," she agreed, running around the corner.

Joe turned back to Sylvie. "Better?"

"Much better."

"I'm not a monster," he insisted.

"I know." He was a man who had his own reasons for resenting the holidays, and she needed to remember that. Sylvie turned and climbed the rest of the stairs to the second floor. She stopped at the foot of the ladder that was placed in front of the bathroom door. Above it was a trapdoor.

"Stand back," he said, moving the ladder into place. He climbed up, pushed the door open, then took two more steps up the ladder to enter the attic.

"Do you want the flashlight now?"

"Yeah." His hand dangled away from her, so Sylvie reached out and touched his sleeve to give him the light. He moved his hand, and their fingers tangled for a brief, surprising moment until he clutched the metal barrel of the flashlight and Sylvie released it to him.

She heard him take a deep breath. "Thanks," he muttered, and climbed the remaining steps of the ladder to disappear inside the attic.

Sylvie put trembling hands on the sides of the

ladder and listened as Joe sneezed. "Do you want me to come up there, too?" When he didn't answer, she repeated her question a little louder.

"Wait!" he called. "I think I found that damn wreath. I'll hand it to you—it's not heavy."

She watched as he lowered a plastic bag out of the attic, and Sylvie reached for it very carefully in order to avoid touching those warm fingers again. From now on she would mind her own business, stay with the children, and avoid personal conversations.

She would be gone in nine days.

"IT'S FOR YOU." Hank held out the phone to Joe, who took it with great reluctance.

"Hello?" He grimaced. This was the third phone call tonight, and all three callers were friends who had either seen the ad themselves or been told about it. Joe took the kidding with good grace, but when he hung up the telephone and returned to his supper, he glanced toward his older niece.

"Looks like plenty of people saw those ads."

She winced. "I'm sorry, Uncle Joe."

"You called the stores and asked them to be removed?"

"Uh-huh." She finished her mouthful of green beans and looked at Sylvie, who had spent the afternoon talking only to the children and to Hank. His house looked like Mrs. Santa herself had prepared it for the old man's arrival.

"Should die down in a day or two," Hank

muttered. "Sylvie, hon, would you pass those biscuits down here again?"

"Sure," she said, looking pleased that Hank wanted seconds. Or was it thirds? Supper consisted of a pretty good meat loaf, baked potatoes, canned green beans and those mouthwatering biscuits. She'd found a container of strawberry jam somewhere and put a fresh stick of butter on a saucer, too. Joe wondered how she'd found the time after draping his house with Christmas paraphernalia. But, hell, that was her "job." She wouldn't last long, probably not even the remaining days until Christmas. She was a drifter, a woman with a car and baby and little else, here today and gone tomorrow. The thought cheered him.

Joe pushed his empty plate aside. "You'd think people would have better things to do during a blizzard than give me a hard time."

Hank split open a biscuit and reached for the butter dish. "You have to admit, it's pretty funny picturing you advertising for a wife. I'll bet the whole town's getting a kick out of this."

"What kind of man would do something like that?" He glanced over to Sylvie. "No offense, but for a man to put up an ad? He'd have to be at least half crazy."

"I don't think so. Perfectly nice men have done it," the woman stated. "It's really not that unusual."

"I saw something on TV," Hank said. "A lawyer—seemed like a nice guy—rented a billboard. He wanted to get married and have kids."

Sylvie nodded. "Did you see the Texas billionaire on *Oprah?* He had the ring and everything, but he was waiting for the right woman."

"Darn," said Hank. "I guess I missed that one."

Joe couldn't believe Hank was going along with this. "This character thought he was going to find the *right woman* on a TV show?"

Sylvie turned those blue eyes on him. "Why not? Nice women watch *Oprah.*"

"That's not what I meant," he began. "I just don't think—"

"People have their reasons for what they do, even if that's not the kind of thing *you* would do," she told him. "You're not very compassionate."

Karen frowned. "What's that mean?"

Peter, seated near his grandfather, helped himself to another biscuit. "I think it's a dress."

"Uncle Joe doesn't wear dresses."

"Pass those biscuits over here," Joe told his niece. "Of course I don't wear dresses. Why would you think a thing like that?"

Janie giggled so hard she dropped her fork. Sylvie got up and retrieved a clean one from the drawer by the sink, then returned to the table. Joe frowned. She didn't have to act like a servant.

"Janie could have done that herself," he said, knowing he sounded like the monster she'd accused him of being earlier. He pointed to the butter dish and Peter pushed it toward him.

"I'm here to help," Sylvie reminded him without meeting his gaze. She looked at Hank instead. "What should I make for Christmas dinner? Do you have a lot of company or do you go somewhere else?"

"A nice roast turkey would be fine," the old man said. "And it's just us. We're kind of a small group."

"Not to me," Sylvie said.

"What about your family? Won't they miss you?" Joe asked.

He might as well have stabbed her with his knife, he realized, as he saw pain flare briefly in those clear blue eyes.

"They're in Paris," she said.

Joe forgot any guilt niggling at his conscience. "Texas?"

"France."

"I see." He saw, as he chewed the best biscuit he'd ever had in his life, that she was a lousy liar. "What are they doing there?"

"Painting." She turned away from his gaze and reached for the platter in front of her. "Does anyone want seconds? There're still a few pieces of meat loaf."

"No, thanks." Hank reached for another biscuit. "My wife never wanted to travel much, but I sure like reading those copies of *National Geographic*. I always thought I'd like to see a rain forest or maybe one of them African game reserves.

Sure would be interesting to see a lion wrestle down a skinny-legged gazelle."

"Are you a hunter?" Sylvie rose and began clearing the table.

"Only when I'm protecting the cattle, but my eyesight's not what it used to be."

"What else—besides turkey—would you like for Christmas dinner?"

Joe noticed she directed the question toward Hank.

"Creamed onions," the man said, smacking his lips with anticipation while his grandchildren made gagging sounds.

"I'll find a recipe," she said. "Anything else?"

Janie bounced up and down in her seat. "Candy-cane cookies."

"Cutout cookies?"

"Brownies!"

"And maybe some of those thumbprint cookies my wife used to make," Hank said, finally pushing his plate aside. "I know I can put my hands on that recipe."

"I'd be glad to," Sylvie said. What else could she say? Joe wondered. It was her job to do Christmas. She'd told him that was what she'd been hired to do, and that fragile appearance hid a stubborn streak. Well, he'd be damned if he could think what he wanted to see on the holiday dinner table. Even if someone asked him. Which no one did. The five of them continued to talk about food while Sylvie and Karen cleared the table and Joe silently poured coffee for Hank.

When the baby awoke and cried for his own supper, the three kids followed Sylvie into the living room. Pretty soon Joe heard "Rudolph the Red-Nosed Reindeer" coming from the stereo.

"Looks like we got us some holiday spirit," Hank drawled.

"Whether we needed it or not?"

"We needed it." The old man's expression grew serious. "We've got to give those kids a holiday like their mother would have given them."

"Sylvie Smith isn't Deb."

Hank wrapped his large hands around his coffee mug and looked down into it as if it held all the answers. "You don't have to tell me that, Joe. I've lost a wife and a daughter and there've been lots of mornings I didn't feel like getting up and facing the day." He lifted sorrow-filled eyes and met Joe's gaze. "Three years ago you lost a brother, but you can't let that make you bitter for the rest of your life."

"I'm doing the best I can."

"Yeah." Hank looked down at his coffee again. "We all are."

"NO WAY."

"I promised the children." Sylvie ordered herself to keep her temper. She was still embarrassed by yesterday's scene on the stairs. It wasn't like her to yell at people—especially men—though in the last two days she'd wondered what she'd say to Billy Ray if she ever found him. Nothing nice, she supposed, though that probably wasn't fair to Dillon. Her son deserved a father. Dillon would want to know his family, if he had grandparents and cousins. She didn't want her son to know the same emptiness that took up too much space in her heart.

She watched as Joe Brockett pulled out a kitchen chair and sat down. He took off heavy leather work gloves and set them on the table, then he unwound a ragged gray scarf from his neck. "You have any idea what the weather's like out there?"

"No." Dillon fussed in her arms. She shifted him so that he lay adjacent to her shoulder, but his little legs squirmed against her breast. "It stopped snowing last night."

"But the wind didn't stop, lady. We've got seven-foot drifts in some places."

"The school bus—"

"Stays on the main roads."

"They'll be home soon, and Janie will be awake from her nap. They're expecting a tree. Surely you must know where to get one."

He leaned back in his chair and acted as if the tree discussion was over. "How old is that baby?"

"*Dillon* is eight weeks old."

"Eight weeks," he repeated, as if he couldn't believe an infant was in his house. "You never said where his father was."

She lifted her chin. She could be as blunt as this rancher. "I can't tell you what I don't know."

She didn't expect the flash of sympathy from

those dark eyes, so she turned away and busied herself with stirring the pan of hot chocolate she'd heated on the stove. There were no marshmallows to float on top, but she was sure the children would like the treat. Someday Dillon would come home from school to drink hot chocolate and tell her about his day, though that was hard to picture as he snuggled against her neck and dreamed baby dreams.

She didn't know Joe was beside her until she smelled his leather coat mixed with the fresh scent of Montana air. She turned, but he blocked her way.

Understanding flashed across the rancher's wind-burned face. "And that's why you came to Willum. To find his father."

"That's none of your business," she began. "I—"

He put one large cool hand on her shoulder. "Give me a name and I'll see what I can do."

"I don't think it's that easy anymore."

His fingers tightened briefly, as if he'd like to shake her, then his hand left her shoulder as if he'd been stung. "Jeez, lady, haven't you figured out that nothing's easy?"

Her arms tightened around Dillon's warm body. "I think I'm starting to catch on," she said, a trace of sarcasm tinting her words. "Could we talk about the tree now?"

"*You* can talk about the tree from now until the snow melts." He picked up his gloves and grabbed the scarf before heading for the door. "I've got work to do."

She followed him onto the chilly back porch. "I'll tell the children to wear long underwear and their thickest gloves. And I'll fix a thermos of hot chocolate."

Her answer was the slam of the back door, but Sylvie didn't mind. When was the last time someone had tried to comfort her, touch her, reach out to her? Her shoulder, strained from carrying Dillon for long hours, still felt the imprint of Joe Brockett's large hand. He had offered to help her find Dillon's father, an offer she appreciated. She didn't know what stopped her from saying Billy Ray's name, except that she didn't want anyone's help. She never expected it and she didn't know what to do when it was offered.

Besides, she'd been distracted. He had touched her, and her skin had warmed at the surprising intimacy.

6

"WHY ARE WE GOING TO town?"

Because I've been bullied by a tiny woman with more holiday spirit than sense, he wanted to tell his nephew, but Joe swiped the condensation off the windshield with his gloved hand and said only, "To get a tree."

"You mean *buy* a tree," Karen declared.

"Whatever."

"Is it wrong to buy one?" the Christmas "fiend" asked in a deceptively innocent voice. "I mean, does it go against tradition?"

Joe shrugged to torture her. "If you want a tree, this is the only way to get one today."

"Then it's going to be just fine," Sylvie declared, and turned around to smile at the children in the back seat. The baby, strapped into his car seat, sat between Karen and Peter, while Janie shared the front seat with the adults. "Right, kids?"

"Right. We hafta get a tree," Janie said, tugging on her uncle's sleeve. "We got all the pretty ornaments for it."

"I like cutting it down," Peter mumbled. "I like holding the saw."

"Your father and I used to fight over who was

going to make the first cut," Joe surprised himself by announcing.

"Who won?"

"He usually did. He was a year older than me, and taller, too."

"My dad was bigger than you?"

"Yeah." He glanced in the rearview mirror and caught the boy's eye. "But every once in a while I could catch him off guard. We liked to wrestle and our mother would scold us."

"You got scolded?" Karen was clearly shocked at the thought of anyone scolding him, and Joe didn't bother to hide his amusement.

"Sure. I was a kid once." Which he had forgotten, he realized. He figured he'd been old for years.

"You've always had Christmas on the ranch, haven't you?"

The fiend again. Joe made sure he kept his gaze on the snow-coated road ahead of him. "Of course. It's my home."

For some reason, that seemed to shut her up until they arrived in town. He turned onto Main Street and took the second left to the supermarket. "Here," he said, pulling into the parking lot and finding an empty place in a corner where the snow had been plowed into hills.

"Uh-oh," Karen muttered.

"What's wrong?" Sylvie turned around.

"It's the scene of the crime," Joe explained as he switched off the engine and unsnapped his seat belt. "I'll be right back." Before he did anything else in town today, he was going to make sure that no other woman driving through Willum, Montana, thought he needed a wife. He slammed the car door shut, then lifted his collar against the wind. It was going to be another cold night; and from the looks of that sky, Joe knew he'd better do his errands and get home before it stormed again. He made his way across the parking lot and into the stuffy supermarket. The blue card was where Karen had said it was, so he removed the thumbtack, stuck it back on the board, and read the same words that Sylvie had read on Saturday. Help Wanted: Wife.

Joe swore under his breath and tossed the card in a nearby wastebasket where it belonged. He'd find the others, too, while he was in town, and put an end to this mess once and for all. There were a lot of things he needed—like a new saddle and a roof for the calving shed—but getting married wasn't one of them. He'd only wanted to get married once, a long time ago, but she'd been in love with someone else and he'd never really worked up much enthusiasm for marriage since then. He'd get the damn tree, he'd smile and act like he was enjoying himself, and then he'd go home and get to work.

There was always enough of that to go around, Christmas or no Christmas.

"WELL?"

Sylvie watched Joe frown as he held the tree away from the others that were leaned against the brick wall of Playhouse Bar. A nearby cardboard sign proclaimed that any and all Christmas trees were twenty dollars. She didn't know what Joe had against Christmas trees, for heaven's sake, but she wished he would at least pretend to be interested. "It's a little thin."

He leaned it back against the others.

"What about this one?" Karen pointed to a tree tall enough to belong in a town hall.

"I think that might be a little big," she told her, hoping she wouldn't hurt the child's feelings.

"We could get it," Joe offered, "but I'd have to take a chain saw to it."

Sylvie decided he wasn't teasing and, tucking Dillon against her chest, headed to a group of trees in the corner of the parking lot. She couldn't stay out here much longer—not with the temperature dropping. "What about one of these?"

Peter jumped up and down and pointed to a forest of green branches stacked against the side of the building. "Over here!"

"No!" hollered Janie from another part of the lot. "Here!"

Joe moved to Sylvie's side. "You and the baby had better get in the car. This could take a while."

"I don't know how we can decide."

"You pick one and they'll be happy."

"They will?"

"Yeah," he said, stomping his feet as if to get the blood pumping to them, "but just don't take too long. I've got animals to feed."

"I don't know which one—"

"Just get one that's not too big. Whatever you get is going to look fine once you hang a few ornaments on it." He took his wallet from his back pocket. "I'll go inside and pay. You've got five minutes."

Sylvie made sure that Dillon's face was concealed from the cold air while she hurried over to Peter. The little boy pointed to a tree that nestled against others. "This one," he said, his chin jutting out in a very determined, very Brockett way. Janie ran over to look.

"It's okay, I guess," the little girl admitted. "Mine's nice, too."

"It's very pretty," Sylvie told them, though she secretly thought most of the trees looked exactly like what Christmas trees should look like: green, bushy triangles of fragrant pine needles. She waved at Karen, who hurried across the parking lot to join them. "What do you think of this one?"

Karen shivered and shoved her hands into her coat pockets. "Do *you* like it, Sylvie?"

"I sure do."

"Me, too," Janie added, leaning against Sylvie's side. "I'm cold."

Peter grinned. "We're gonna get *my* tree?"

"Yes. Can you and Karen carry it to the car? Your uncle went inside to pay."

"Maybe we can drag it," Karen said, as her brother reached through the branches to grab the trunk.

"It's awfully heavy," the boy admitted as the tree swayed to one side.

"Stop," came the order from across the lot. Joe hurried toward them. "I'll take care of it," he said. "Everyone get in the car."

Peter's face fell. "Even me?"

"No," his uncle said. "I was talking to the women."

Sylvie tried not to smile as she led the shivering girls to the car. Peter may not have had the fun of cutting down the tree, but carrying it back to the Jeep must be the next best thing. From the car's warm interior they watched as Joe produced a rope and somehow managed to secure the tree on top of the car. Men's work, obviously, Sylvie thought as she turned her attention back to her son. Dillon slept peacefully, unaware that he was missing out on something so testosterone-inspired.

Karen leaned forward. "Can we have hot chocolate now?"

"Sure. Can you pour it for you and Janie?"

"Yep."

"We can pretend we're out in the woods," Sylvie told the girls, twisting around to make certain they were careful with the hot drinks.

"I like pretending," the older girl agreed. "Sometimes it works out."

"Sometimes," Sylvie cautioned, glancing down at her son. She'd pretended a lot of things this past year, until reality had struck with a sudden and chilling blow. Billy Ray didn't live in this town, and in her pathetic enthusiasm to find Dillon a father she'd ended up endangering them both. "If it's just for fun."

Janie, her red hat dangerously close to falling off, frowned. "Can I pretend you're my mommy?"

"No, honey, I don't think that would be a very good idea."

Karen stared at her over the rim of her plastic cup. "Just for Christmas?"

Sylvie shook her head. "Instead of pretending, why don't we all agree that I'm really—really and *truly*—your friend?"

The girls didn't look happy or convinced, but they didn't have a chance to protest because Peter and their uncle joined them in the car. Joe looked at the hot chocolate and glanced pointedly at his watch.

"We don't have a lot of time," he said.

"We're pretending we're in the woods," Karen told him, handing her brother a cup. "You want some, Uncle Joe?"

"No, thanks. I've still got some errands to do." He adjusted his seat belt and looked in the rearview mirror. "The three of you can hold on to your drinks?"

"Yeah," Peter said. "It's not real hot."

"I've got to get the rest of those ads," Joe explained, starting up the car. "I'm already the laughingstock of the town."

"I'm sorry, Uncle Joe," Karen said. "But you know? It kinda worked out, because now we have Sylvie."

Sylvie was the only one who could see the man wince, but she didn't feel the least bit sorry for him. She had decided to be nice to him during this excursion. For the children's sake. To give him credit, he'd been patient and he was the only one to have thought about bringing a rope. "Thank you for the tree," she said, and was surprised when he glanced toward her and half smiled.

"No problem," he said, turning his attention back to the road. "I'm glad it's over with."

"HERE," RUBY SAID, handing Hank a blue index card. "I took it off the diner window this morning. Those grandchildren of yours must really be something."

"They meant well." Hank glanced at the card, then tucked it into his shirt pocket. "Can I buy you a cup of coffee?" He told himself he was only being polite. The woman had done him a favor, after all, and Joe would be relieved to have one less ad displayed in town. "Unless you have work to do."

She looked at her watch, a thick band of silver and turquoise. "I have a little while before my next perm."

"Well," was all he could think of to say as he followed her over to one of the red booths under a window that faced Main Street. She wore a bright pink parka with a hood trimmed with fluffy white fur, and her black jeans were tucked into waterproof white boots. She should have looked out of place, but when she scooted into the booth and smiled at him, Hank figured pink was a pretty nice color.

"I'm glad I ran into you," she said, unzipping

her jacket to reveal a silky white blouse. A silver necklace draped around her neck and disappeared into an ample cleavage. "I was on my way to the post office to mail bills, but this is more fun."

She smelled like roses. Hank sat against the back of the booth and tried not to bump his legs against hers. Darn, he wasn't used to being around strange women. Not that Ruby was strange, but hell. She looked at him like he was single, for Pete's sake. And that was a pretty damn strange feeling for a man his age. "I had some errands in town," he managed to say.

"Christmas shopping?" She smiled at him and then at the yellow-haired waitress who came to take their order. "Hi, Meg. I'll just have a cup of coffee, please."

"Sure thing. Hank?"

"Coffee. Black."

"No pie? We've got some killer pumpkin pie today and real whip cream," the young lady offered.

"Not for me," Ruby said. "Hank?"

"Ah, no killer pie for me, either."

Ruby turned back to Meg. "Are you letting that perm grow out or are you going to need another before New Year's Eve, honey?"

"I had to put a new clutch in my truck, so the only way I'm gettin' my hair done is if my mom gives me a gift certificate to the Hair Hut for Christmas."

"She's coming in for a shampoo and set tomorrow, so I'll give her a hint. I've got some makeover specials, too."

"Thanks, Ruby." The waitress shoved her pad back into the apron of her striped uniform. "I'll hurry right back with your coffee."

"No hurry," Hank lied. He wondered what the hell he was doing, sitting in the middle of town looking for all the world like he was courting Ruby Dee. Not that a man wouldn't be proud to be seen with her, but widowed ranchers just weren't the woman's type.

"So, you buying those grandchildren of yours some toys today?"

"Yeah, I've got a few things in the truck."

"You have three, right?"

He nodded as Meg set their coffee mugs on the table. "Just holler when you want a refill or if you change your mind about the pie," the girl said before she hurried back to the counter.

"Two girls and a boy," Hank said. "My daughter's kids."

"I moved here right before she died," Ruby said, her voice soft. "She seemed like a sweet girl, though I only met her a couple of times."

"You did her hair for the funeral. I never did thank you, but that was real nice."

"I was glad I could do something to help." Ruby looked away and took a sip of her coffee. "Tell me what you bought those kids of yours."

Grateful to change the subject, Hank tried to explain how many times he'd walked the toy aisle of the hardware store. "I should have holes in my boots," he declared, tickled when Ruby smiled at him again. "The boys are easy, but I sure don't know much about girls."

"Bring them to the Hut for a manicure. I'd have fun fussing over them."

"They're awfully young for a beauty parlor."

"How young?"

"Four and eleven."

"Old enough," she declared. "You come to the shop and I'll do up some nice gift certificates that you can put in their stockings."

"Sounds good," Hank said, taking another swallow of coffee. He was starting to enjoy himself. "You have grandchildren?"

"No." Sadness flickered in those blue eyes for a second, but she fiddled with her coffee cup and glanced out the window. "Looks like everyone's getting their Christmas trees this week. It seems like every time I look out my window I see someone else going by with a tree sticking out of their truck. It sure is a happy time of year."

"We've got the spirit out at the ranch. A nice little gal answered that ad my granddaughter spread around town and she—"

"Joe Brockett's getting married?" Ruby began to laugh. "I don't believe it."

"Aw, hell, Ruby, it's not like that at all. She's a sweet young lady with no place to go and a baby and all, so I kinda hired her to stay for Christmas and do all that stuff that women do to make things nice."

"You're a good man, Hank Cavendish." She

reached out and patted his large, veined hand with her soft fingers. "You have a good heart."

He didn't move his hand. He told himself that was because he hadn't felt a woman's touch in years, that was all. "It's no hardship on me and Joe. Sylvie's a good cook. And real good with the kids."

"I'd like to meet her. Tell her to come by the Hut and say hello the next time she's in town."

"She's pretty tied down with the baby and all."

Ruby looked disappointed, leaving Hank to worry that he'd somehow hurt her feelings. It was all coming back to him, how women were real sensitive and all. He hurried to make her smile at him again. "You could come out to the ranch," he heard himself offer. "Those kids are sure excited about decorating a Christmas tree this year."

Ruby looked at him as if he'd handed her the moon, with a couple of stars thrown in for sparkle. "Really? You're inviting me?"

"Well, sure." He couldn't take it back now, and he didn't know if he wanted to. "I'll ask Sylvie if she'll make something special for Sunday dinner, if you're free then."

"Church gets out at eleven."

Hank nodded. He knew how women felt about church. "You want me to pick you up?"

She gave him a strange look. "I can drive," she said slowly.

"Roads could be bad. You got four-wheel?"

"Front-wheel. It gets me around town most days."

"I'll pick you about eleven-thirty." He hesitated, feeling he should warn her. "It gets pretty noisy around the house, with the kids being excited and all."

She smiled. "I like noise. That house of mine is too quiet."

"Well," Hank said, finishing his coffee, "guess I've kept you long enough."

"I enjoyed it, Hank. I spend all day talking to women. It was nice to sit and talk with a man for a change."

"Well," he said, pulling out his worn wallet and tossing two dollars on the table.

"Next time you're in town, the coffee will be my treat," she said.

Next time. That didn't sound too bad, though Hank's stomach clenched at the thought of entertaining on Sunday. Aw, hell, he thought, following her out onto the street and watching her head toward the corner. What had he gotten himself into?

A RUBY GLASS BALL FELL to the floor and, before Sylvie could retrieve it, was crunched beneath the rocking chair as Hank rocked backward.

"Well, shoot," he said, stopping his rendition of "Frosty the Snowman." "What the heck was that?"

"Another ornament," Sylvie explained as she grabbed the dustpan and broom for the third time.

"You kids be more careful," their grandfather said, as he sat contentedly in the midst of chaos. Dillon fussed on the old man's lap, but Hank didn't seem to mind. He scooted the chair out of the way while Sylvie attempted to sweep up the pile of broken glass before the children stepped in it.

"We are," Peter assured him, a delicate crystal icicle clutched like a sword in his hand.

The tree decorating hadn't been the warm and cozy event Sylvie had envisioned. Forget the soft holiday music, bayberry candles, glistening decorations and pine-scented fir of those fantasy Christmases of her childhood. Janie had insisted on playing "Frosty" over and over again, in order to prove to everyone that she had learned the words for her preschool's performance next week. Glowing candles would have set the room—and its rambunctious occupants—on fire. The glass bulbs were too fragile for eager young fingers and the tree smelled suspiciously as if a dog or two had used it as a fire hydrant.

Sylvie sniffed again, then wished she hadn't. She'd asked Joe to build a fire in the fireplace and now the heat seemed to be activating whatever coated the lower branches of their beautiful tree.

"Is that darn thing listing to the left again?"

Sylvie turned to see Joe standing in the doorway. She looked back at the tree and cocked her head. "I can't tell. Maybe."

"Jeez," he sputtered, then disappeared.

"Don't mind him," Hank said. "He's probably just hungry."

She should tell him there were leftover chicken and potatoes in the refrigerator, but she'd bet he could probably figure that out by himself.

Janie picked up a stuffed fabric candy cane and dangled it from a branch at nose height. "The lights are so pretty," the child said, sighing.

And that was another thing, Sylvie thought, dropping the remnants of the ornament into a paper bag filled with trash. No one had told her that stringing lights around a tree brought out the worst in a person. She had almost—almost—yelled at Peter when he'd wound a newly untangled string of lights around his waist and pretended to be trapped by "bad guys from outer space."

When Joe returned with a fistful of heavy twine and a hammer, Janie burst into tears. "You can't take my tree!"

Joe stared down at her. "Honey, I'm not taking the tree anywhere. But I have to make sure it doesn't fall over."

Sylvie put her arm around the little girl. "Fall over?"

"Yeah," the man said. "You don't want to wake up one morning and find that the tree's gone horizontal on you, right?"

"Of course not."

"Well," he said, grabbing one of the kitchen

chairs they'd used for a ladder, "let me make sure."

"Okay," Janie agreed, watching her uncle's every move. "You won't hurt my tree?"

"Nope. I promise. Everyone get out of the way, will you?"

As everyone did as they were told, Hank leaned forward and handed Sylvie her fussing child. "I think he's ready for a new diaper."

"Thanks for holding him."

"My pleasure," the old man replied. "Been too long since we had a baby around here." He turned to Joe. "You want help?"

"No, I'm just going to run a line or two." He banged some nails into the wall, then wound twine from the top of the tree to the nails. The ornaments shook, but nothing else fell off the branches. "This'll be fine."

It looked a little strange—nothing like a Martha Stewart production—but Sylvie supposed that Martha had never dealt with a practical Montana rancher, either. Once the room was dark and the tree lights were on, no one would notice the twine that anchored the tree to the wall. And the children would be sitting around the tree opening presents, so the odd additions to the tree wouldn't show in the Christmas-morning pictures.

"Do you have a camera?" Sylvie asked, suddenly realizing that this holiday needed to be recorded—for all of them. She could prove to Dillon that his first Christmas had been something to remember, complete with a tree and presents and a grandfather in a rocking chair.

"Somewhere," Joe muttered, climbing down from the chair. He backed up and eyed his handiwork. "That's better. Sturdy."

Hank grinned. "You expecting a storm or something?"

"Just making sure it's safe."

Safe. Now there was a novel concept. Sylvie swallowed hard as the tree shimmered in unshed tears. She and Dillon were safe, she reminded herself, holding the baby's soft head against her shoulder. At least for now. They had a warm place to live and plenty of food, they were out of the wind and snow and inside a home that smelled like—well, that *would* smell like cinnamon after she baked a couple of apple pies tomorrow morning.

Joe inhaled. "What the he—heck is that smell?"

She leaned closer to him. "I think it's the tree, but don't say anything or you'll hurt Peter's feelings."

He kept his voice low, but he looked as if he wanted to laugh. "Why? Did *he* pee on it?"

"Of course not." Sylvie adjusted her hold on Dillon, who picked that time to scream his desire for a late supper. "But he picked it out, and he'll take it personally if you criticize how bad it smells."

"Like an outhouse," he grumbled, but he gave the kids a big smile. "That tree sure looks good."

Janie wrapped her arms around his knees. "I love my tree."

"It's not just yours," her brother told her. He stood beside his uncle and stared at the tree. "I think it's real straight now."

Hank eased himself out of the rocker and switched off the lamp by the chair, leaving the room lit only by the multicolored blinking lights. "Well, that sure is a pretty sight."

Karen let out a sigh. "This is the best Christmas ever," she said, hugging her grandfather.

Hank winked at Sylvie, who rubbed Dillon's soft cheek with her own. Temporarily distracted by the lights, he peered over his mother's shoulder to gaze at the tree.

"Dillon likes it," Janie announced.

"He's never seen a Christmas tree before," Sylvie said. "I think he's very impressed."

"We all are," Joe Brockett declared, surprising Sylvie with the sincerity in his voice. She glanced at him quickly, then gave him a shy smile. Surely a man who tolerated such a mess couldn't be all bad. But then again, she wasn't a very good judge of men. And she had the baby to prove it.

Karen caught up with her. "Where are you going?"

"To take care of Dillon for a minute."

"And then you'll come back?"

Joe clasped the child's shoulder. "Sylvie's not going anywhere," he said, his voice low. "Let her be."

Sylvie stepped away from the cozy family

scene. After all, she had a diaper to change. She certainly had no business smiling at a good-looking rancher who occasionally showed a little charm. She had no use for charm. And no use for men, no matter how nicely they smiled or whatever words they spoke to make a woman feel like she was special—and, God help her, loved. She was through with love. What she needed was a job and nothing else.

THE SOUND OF CRYING woke him. With his eyes still closed, Joe listened but couldn't tell if he heard the infant or Janie. He hadn't heard Sylvie's child before, since he was a man who slept hard and deep. Even during those long months after Deb and Jim had died, he'd worked eighteen hours a day to make sure he'd have no nightmares, no midnight pain.

Listening to a child's sobs was something different, even if the sound was something he'd heard before in the middle of the night. He rolled out of bed and pulled on a pair of jeans, then hurried down the hall to Janie's room, where only silence and his niece's rhythmic breathing greeted him when he opened the door. No, the cries came from the kitchen.

He didn't stop to figure out why he went downstairs instead of heading back to his bed—except that he remembered his brother's tender care of his wife in those months after they'd had a child. Jim hadn't been at all reluctant to get up in the middle of the night to change diapers and help his tired wife deal with a baby's demands.

She stood by the kitchen table, a stranger in Deb's territory. He waited for the familiar resentment to surface, but this time he only felt sorry for Sylvie. There was something about the woman. He stepped closer and, when she turned to look at him, he noticed her eyelashes were fringed with tears. She was barefoot; a faded gray sweatshirt hung loosely over a knee-length nightgown. She had no right to look so vulnerable that all he wanted to do was take her into his arms.

"You okay?"

"I'm sorry we woke you," she whispered, patting the child's back. "Dillon won't stop crying. I don't know why."

"Is he sick?"

"I don't know. He just ate and then he started crying like his heart was broken."

Joe held out his arms. "Give him to me."

"Why?"

"I'll walk him. Burp him. Something."

"You don't know how."

"There are three kids upstairs, honey." He didn't tell her that he had been more of an observer than a participant in their care when they were babies. But hell, she didn't have to know everything. "I've seen my brother deal with babies, and there didn't seem to be much to it besides walking around and singing some Willie Nelson song." Sylvie reluctantly handed him her son, and he gathered the protesting child against his shoulder. He smelled like baby powder and sweet milk, but his little legs were rigid against Joe's bare chest. "Okay, kid, calm down."

"No song?"

He should have put on a shirt. Joe tried to remember if he'd zipped up his jeans. "I'm tone-deaf."

"Dillon wouldn't know the difference."

"Yeah, he would." The child bunched his legs up and howled. "I think the little fella has gas."

"Is that the same as colic?"

"Sometimes, I guess, but maybe he just needs to walk around."

"That's what I've been doing."

"And crying along with him, from the looks of you."

She surprised him by smiling. "I tried to be a little quieter than my son."

He did a few laps around the kitchen, then sauntered into the hall to the dark living room. Sylvie followed him, as he knew she would, until they stood in front of the tree. She knelt down by the wall and plugged in the lights, which gave the room a festive glow, and Dillon's sobs hiccuped to a halt.

Joe kept patting the kid's back, though. He wasn't about to risk torturing his eardrums again. He raised his eyebrows as he caught Sylvie's expression of relief. She shrugged, obviously afraid that the sound of her voice would start another crying fit. Joe stood in front of the tree and continued to pat the kid's back until the baby slumped in his arms and his breathing became even.

"Now what?" Sylvie mouthed.

"Bed?" It shouldn't have sounded like such an intimate question. Joe dropped his gaze and concentrated on the swirl of golden hair that topped Dillon's crown. He had his mother's coloring, but who was his father? And why wasn't he around to take care of his family? Joe thrust aside an uncomfortable stab of anger and turned toward the door.

Sylvie, her arms reaching for her child, was at Joe's side in a heartbeat. "I'll take him."

"No, I'll do it," he whispered. "He might wake up if we move him too much. Don't worry about the tree. I'll come back down and get the lights." Lord, he sounded domestic. He guessed that was what came of having a baby in the house; of having a woman in the house. He followed her up the stairs and down to the end of the hall to what had, up until a few days ago, been Karen's room. Now it held Sylvie's meager possessions: an old little playpen, a plastic car seat, an assortment of worn suitcases and several boxes of disposable diapers.

He gave her the child, making a careful effort to put the baby into Sylvie's arms without touching an inch more of the woman than was absolutely necessary. He had no business being attracted to her. He had no reason to want to touch her—no reason except that it had been such a long time since he'd touched a woman, and, as he reminded himself, she was nothing like Deb.

Which could be a good thing, if he had half a

brain to consider that. He didn't want to feel desire for this woman—especially not in Deb's house. Instead, he watched as Sylvie gently eased her son into his makeshift bed, adjusted his faded blue blanket and backed slowly away.

Suddenly the room seemed too small. Joe was conscious of his bare chest and Sylvie's bare toes. There was a softness about the woman, something mysterious and appealing to a rough-living man who'd been alone for too long. Who would think that baby powder was arousing, or that the sight of a tousle-haired woman in a Washington Huskies sweatshirt would make him wonder what was beneath those layers of cotton?

She stumbled and he reached out to steady her. His hands held her upright and suddenly she was tucked against him. Neither one of them moved for the space of a heartbeat, until she turned in his arms to look up at him.

He should have stopped, he realized later—much later. He should have removed his hands from her upper arms and backed away. He should never have dropped his gaze to her lips, or lowered his head. Or touched his mouth to hers.

She was very, very soft. And surprisingly yielding, as if she wasn't thinking, either. He had grown hard with an urgency that made him ache against the restraining denim fabric of his jeans. He had been careful not to touch her with his body even as the kiss lengthened into something more than a casual mistake in the middle of the night. He wanted her with a force he hadn't known existed, with a passion he hadn't realized he would have for another woman.

He didn't know who had stopped it. He didn't care. When they had separated—there in the darkness of his niece's room, with a baby's soft breathing the only other sound—Joe only knew that he had to leave her or make love to her. So he had left, but he wasn't sure how he had managed to get back into his own room and with oddly shaking hands shut the door.

He was a fool to have touched her in the first place.

7

HAVING SYLVIE WAS THE next best thing to having a mom. Karen stepped into the warm kitchen and smelled something really yummy cooking in the oven. Even Peter and Janie had told her she'd been right about putting that ad up in town, even if Uncle Joe was still cranky about the whole "sorry business," as he called it. Her personal Christmas miracle was getting better and better.

Sylvie, her face smudged with flour, popped up from behind the counter and set a large bowl by the sink. "Hi, Karen. How was school?"

"Fine." Karen hoped her mom wouldn't be mad if they all liked Sylvie and wished she'd stay forever.

"Where's Peter?"

"Talking to Grandpa. What are you making?"

"More cookies, I hope." She made a face. "Janie just went to wash up. I let her help roll out the dough for the sugar cookies."

"And I missed it?" Karen started to close the door, but Uncle Joe stepped inside and shook the snow off his hat.

"There's lots left to do, don't worry."

"Don't worry about what?" Uncle Joe asked, closing the door behind him.

Sylvie turned to peer into the oven. "Cookies," was all she said as she got really busy fiddling with the pot holders.

Karen sat down at the table and dumped her backpack by her feet. "I didn't want to miss out. This is the best part of Christmas."

Her uncle poured himself a cup of coffee and leaned against the doorjamb. "I thought the damn tree was."

"Not anymore," she replied, figuring he was teasing again. Sometimes it was hard to tell, but this afternoon he gave her a wink. Just like Grandpa would, if he was here. "Did my mom and dad love each other?"

Uncle Joe looked down at his boots for a minute, then at her. "Why would you ask a question like that?"

Karen shrugged. "I just wondered why people get married, that's all—" and if somehow she could get Uncle Joe and Sylvie to get married and stay together. "I'm doing a report for school," she fibbed, crossing her fingers under the table.

"For school?" Joe frowned. "When I was in fifth grade we were still doing fractions."

Sylvie opened the oven door and pulled a tray of golden star-shaped cookies from inside. She set them on top of the stove and began to transfer them to a cooling rack.

"Sylvie?" Karen asked. "Can you help me?"

She shook her head. "Sorry, honey, but I'm the wrong person to ask about marriage."

"Didn't you ever want to get married?"

The stricken look on Sylvie's face told Karen she'd gone too far, but it was too late to take the words back.

"Karen, that's enough," Uncle Joe warned. "Go to your—"

"No," Sylvie interrupted, her face flushed from the stove. "It's okay." She looked at Karen, who wanted to hide under the table. "Of course I wanted to get married. But sometimes things don't always work out the way you plan them to. Which I guess is a good lesson even if you're only in fifth grade."

Karen thought about that for a moment. "But what about love?"

"You can't always plan that, either," she said. "Love just…happens."

"How?"

Sylvie shrugged. "I don't know. I'm better at cooking than I am with relationships."

Joe reached out to sample one of the cookies on the rack. "And we're real glad you are."

"Joe!" Sylvie laughed.

"Ow!"

"Serves you right," she said, moving the cookies out of his reach. "We're going to frost these for Christmas."

"We can't eat them till next week?"

"No."

Janie ran into the room, knocking Uncle Joe closer to the counter and to Sylvie. Karen watched them standing near each other and figured that with a little more time, maybe things would work out just the way she wanted them to. She had eight days until Christmas.

And if she got some help, eight days should be enough.

"FIRST YOU USE A KNIFE to spread on the frosting, then you take a wooden toothpick, like this." Sylvie dipped the toothpick into a small bowl of red frosting and then dragged it across the center of the cookie. "See? Now Santa has a belt."

Janie giggled and bent over the cookie while Joe and Peter looked on. Within seconds Peter leaned closer and began decorating a reindeer while Karen, keeping her cookies out of harm's way, sat at the other end of the table to decorate them.

Sylvie moved away to finish assembling the chicken tortilla casserole she planned to serve for dinner tonight. She glanced at the clock above the refrigerator. Dillon would wake anytime now, and then the next hours would be spent trying to juggle the demands of her job with the demands of her son.

She wished Joe would leave the kitchen, but he'd poured himself another cup of coffee and sat down to read the paper. The only thing he'd said was, "Wind's picking up again. Looks like snow."

Of course, what else could be said after Karen's questions on love and marriage.

Talk about bad timing.

Of course, she would pretend that it never happened. What else could she do? Certainly not waste time weaving romantic daydreams from such a simple thing as a kiss. A kiss shouldn't upset her—not after everything else she'd been through in the past year.

Why, she could almost forget all about it, if she kept busy enough. There would be no foolish thoughts of "happily ever after." She was through with men. Through with sex, certainly. Not that she wished she didn't have her sweet Dillon; but she was wiser now.

Too wise to kiss Joe Brockett again, even if she'd liked it the first time.

"Well, well," Hank drawled, coming in from the back porch. "Sure smells good in here." He peered over Janie's shoulder. "Looks like everyone is gettin' ready for Christmas."

Joe looked up. "Did you check the horses?"

"Sure did. That old mare is starting to perk up."

"Is it snowing yet?"

Hank shrugged out of his denim jacket and hung it over the back of a chair. "Just about."

Sylvie poured a cup of coffee and set it in front of him.

"Thanks, Sylvie."

"You're welcome."

Hank looked at Peter's reindeer. "Guess we got us some good-looking cookies. Can I have a bite?"

His grandson looked horrified. "No way, Grandpa. Not till next week."

"I already tried," Joe said.

"Here," Sylvie said, gathering together the broken cookies and putting them on a plate. She set it in between the men. "Just don't ruin your dinner."

"I like having a woman around the house," Hank declared. "Don't you, Joe?"

Sylvie waited for Joe's answer while she went back to shredding a block of Cheddar cheese. He didn't like having her around. He'd made that clear enough, and yet she knew darn well that she was a big help to him.

"Sylvie's a fine cook," came Joe's reply.

"I think that's the first nice thing you've ever said to me," Sylvie dared. "Does this mean you're getting into the Christmas spirit after all?"

"It means I'm a practical man who appreciates good food." He smiled as he said it, and Sylvie had to look away. He was handsome, after all, and she couldn't help noticing that fact on those rare occasions when he didn't look as if he had the weight of the world on his broad shoulders.

"Why haven't you ever married, then?"

The words were out before she could take them back, but Hank was the one who answered the question. "Ranching's a hard life for a woman," he said. "Long hours, not much money, the isolation... I guess not too many women want to take on old cowboys like us. Right, Joe?"

Sylvie didn't believe it for a minute, but she

was more than ready to change the subject and avoid any more embarrassment. She didn't want Joe to think that she was desperate to marry him—the way she'd appeared when she'd arrived on his doorstep. And she certainly didn't want him to think that she thought—after one kiss—that she had a future here.

"Look, Uncle Joe." Janie held up her Santa Claus cookie. "Isn't it pretty?"

"Why, it sure is."

"I'm gonna save it for Santa. For Christmas Eve." She set it carefully on the table. "Do you think he'll like it?"

"Sure, he will," her uncle said. "What man wouldn't like cookies after a long cold night outside?"

Sylvie smiled. "If that's a hint, forget it. You're not getting any more."

"No?" He smiled into her eyes and held her gaze. "Never?"

Maybe he wasn't talking about cookies. "That's right. Never."

"You're a cruel woman," the man replied, those dark eyes crinkling at the corners.

"Don't think you can sweet-talk me," she said, looking away and pretending to read the recipe from the cookbook. Of course he could sweet-talk her. She was a sitting duck, a woman with no sense when it came to men, especially men in Stetsons. She'd been duped once. It wasn't going to happen again. She had to remember that she was only here until Christmas.

After that, well, she'd be on her way.

And her heart would still be in one piece.

"SYLVIE, YOU SIT IN THE middle," Hank said. "So you can see."

Joe shifted his legs so he wouldn't touch Sylvie's, but it was no use. They were crammed, along with all the other grandparents and parents in Willum, into the elementary-school cafeteria and there was barely room to take off his jacket without hitting the old lady on his left in the eye.

He noticed that Sylvie was equally careful to avoid touching him, but at one point her right knee brushed his left thigh, leaving him with the uncomfortable feeling that he should have stayed home. Where it was safe. Where a man could walk out of the room if he got aroused by something so trivial as the touch of a woman's knee.

He never should have kissed her. Days later he still regretted it, though every once in a while he thought about doing it again. Her lips had been sweet under his, yielding with a soft warmth that had made him ache.

He had no business aching for a woman with no past except for a sleeping baby that she held in her arms. There'd been no warrants out for her arrest, no history of crime, according to the sheriff's office. But Joe didn't believe for two seconds that her parents were painting in Paris, France.

She was a runaway, plain and simple. And

she'd run right into the one place that needed her. *Damn the woman.*

"Excuse me," she whispered, attempting to slip her arm from her jacket. Lord, he hated that thing. It looked like something she must have picked up free from the Salvation Army. Surely no one would ever have paid money for it. And the damn thing couldn't be warm.

"Here," he grumbled, easing the coat from her shoulder. "Let me help."

"No, I can—"

He guided the sleeve down her arm, at the same time wondering what it would be like to undress her, to ease the rest of her clothes from that compact little body and see what was beneath the shapeless sweatshirt she'd worn this morning or the old blue sweater she wore tonight. Sylvie shivered.

"Thank you," she said, wriggling out of the other side of her jacket. She adjusted the sleeping baby in her lap. On the other side of her, Hank gabbed with everyone who walked by, but Joe kept silent—even when three of his friends looked over and waved. He saw Sylvie get some curious looks from some of the people in town, but folks wouldn't think she was with him. At least, he hoped they wouldn't connect Sylvie with that damn ad. He didn't want anyone to say anything to embarrass her.

"Hey there, Brockett," said the elderly woman to his right. "Thought that was you."

Joe reluctantly turned and greeted his neighbors. "How'd you make out during that storm last week?"

"Didn't lose too many, but I was lucky. You?"

"Just a few."

"Hey, I heard you were looking for a wife." Mrs. Johnson eyed him as if he was going to run away. "You have any luck?"

"The kids—"

"Need a mother, yep." She nodded. "I still can't believe Jim and Deb are gone. Seems like yesterday the three of you were buying calves from me for 4-H club."

A hundred years ago. "That's right."

"I always thought you'd be the Brockett who'd marry Debbie Cavendish, though. Guess your brother beat you to it."

"He sure did." Joe said the words with a polite smile, but was saved from having to say anything else when the lights dimmed and the curtains onstage parted to reveal the preschool class. The familiar "Frosty the Snowman" was sung with great gusto by most of the little kids. Janie didn't look the least bit nervous. She even waved at her grandfather after the first verse.

"Guess your brother beat you to it." I never got over it! he wanted to shout. *She married my best friend!*

But that wasn't the worst of it, because all those years he'd never stopped loving her. Oh, he figured she knew. Or guessed. But Jim never did. Joe had been careful to hide how he felt. He'd dated a few local women from time to time. He'd acted interested, had even gone to bed with two or three who'd been more than willing to agree to a short-term relationship with no strings attached. But he'd never fallen in love with any of them.

Because he'd been in love with Deb Cavendish since he was thirteen. He'd even picked out the ring. He'd planned to ask her on New Year's Eve, when the families on the old road traditionally got together for a potluck dinner.

Only Jim had asked her first, the week before Christmas. And she'd said yes. And that was when Joe realized he didn't know anything about women. Fourteen years ago sometimes seemed like only a few minutes.

Joe realized the crowd was applauding, so he put his hands together and clapped for his younger niece. He was glad he wasn't sitting beside Hank after all. This way, they could both pretend they weren't missing Jim and Deb and wishing they were here to see the kids.

Each class had a turn at performing a song or a holiday skit. Peter's kindergarten class sang "All I Want for Christmas Is My Two Front Teeth." Every time they sang the word "two" they stuck two fingers in the air. The audience chuckled as a couple of the children held up one finger instead.

Karen's class did a complicated rendition of "The Twelve Days of Christmas," with Karen as one of the "maids a-milking." They received an extra-long round of applause, and then the sixth grade led everyone in some carols. During "Jingle Bells," Dillon decided he couldn't sleep with so much noise. Sylvie brought him to her shoulder and patted him gently as everyone stood to sing "Silent Night."

Joe turned to offer her a hand and saw tears running down her cheeks. "Sylvie?"

She glanced at him and looked back to the stage. "I'm fine. I was just thinking.... Never mind."

He handed her a handkerchief. "It's clean," he said, then realized she'd washed and ironed it. "Are you homesick?"

She shook her head, then he watched as her eyes filled up with tears again. "I just wish their parents were here to see how wonderful they are."

He didn't stop to think. It was natural to put his arm around her and hold her against his side until the song was finally over. Would the pain of losing Jim and Deb ever go away? Would the guilt of loving his brother's wife ever leave him?

"HONEY, I'VE GOT A little problem."

Sylvie, curled up on the couch with Dillon, looked up to see Hank standing in front of the Christmas tree. This was one of her favorite times of the day, when she could pretend that the house was her home, and the tree that glowed with its hundred lights belonged to her and Dillon. The baby remained fascinated with the colored lights; she'd had to remind him it was time to nurse. She made sure the blanket covered the baby during his midnight feeding. "You're up late, Hank."

"Well, I came over to talk to you kinda private-like." He sat down on the edge of the recliner. "It's about Sunday."

"What's happening on Sunday? Is something special going on?"

A pained expression crossed his square face. "No. I mean, yes." He ran his hands over his knees. "I guess I'm putting in a request for Sunday dinner. I'm having... Well, we're having company."

"Okay. How many people?"

"Just one. A lady."

A lady. Of course. Joe had invited a woman to dinner. Sylvie fussed with Dillon's blanket and kept her voice casual. "Someone special?"

"Someone from town. Uh, she's looking forward to meeting you."

"Why?"

"She heard about the wife ad."

"Oh." She looked at Hank. "Was she someone who wanted to apply for the job?"

The old man flushed. "Oh, she was just teasin', that's all."

Right.

"She's a nice lady," he continued, as if he had to explain.

"Have she and Joe been seeing each other long?"

He stared at her. "Huh?"

"Have she and Joe—"

"Gawd, no," Hank groaned, gripping his hands together. "Ruby's coming up here because I invited her. She's too, uh, old for Joe and too young for me, but I sort of asked her out to the ranch for Sunday dinner by accident, while we were having coffee at the café, and then—"

"Hank." Sylvie couldn't believe the relief that swept through her. "You don't have to explain anything to me. I'm happy to cook anything you want, anytime."

He continued as if she hadn't said a word. "I was married to my Laura for thirty-seven years. I'm surely not looking for another woman. There was only one like my Laura, you know."

Sylvie wanted to cry, but she didn't want to make Hank feel any worse, so she took a deep breath. "I wish I had met her."

"Well, she was a fine woman." Hank sighed.

"Tell me about Sunday. What time do you want dinner?"

"Around one, I guess. You don't have to cook anything fancy. She's just a regular person."

"She lives in town?"

"Runs the beauty salon." He stood and turned to the tree. "Sure looks nice in here. Festive."

"You didn't have a tree last year?"

"We did, but our hearts just weren't in it."

"Are they now?"

Hank turned back toward her. "I had a good idea hiring you, honey. You've done a real good job, too."

"Thanks. But I don't think Joe feels the same way."

"Sure he does," the old man assured her. "He just doesn't know it yet."

Much later, when Dillon slept in his little bed and the house was dark and silent, Sylvie tiptoed downstairs to fix herself a cup of herbal tea and plan what she would cook on Sunday. She would make a menu, starting with tomorrow night, when the kids were finished with school for ten days. Then Saturday. And Sunday. Wednesday was Christmas, Thursday she'd clean and pack, and would be gone first thing Friday. A week from tomorrow—which was a lifetime or only a second, depending on how she thought about it. She took several thick cookbooks from the shelf above the stove and stacked them on the table.

"What are you doing?"

She raised her head, wondering why she was so glad to hear his voice. "I couldn't sleep."

"You don't get enough rest as it is." Joe approached the table and flipped open one of the cookbooks. "Deb Brockett" was written inside the front cover.

"Was she a good cook?"

"She was good at a lot of things." He wore a flannel shirt this time, though he hadn't buttoned it properly. He was barefoot, his jeans rumpled as if he'd picked them up off the floor. She had peeked into his room once and seen chaos.

"Oh." She'd been jealous tonight. Jealous of a woman she didn't even know just because she thought that woman was coming to the ranch to be with Joe. And now she was jealous of a dead woman—a woman married to his brother. Could she get any more pathetic?

He shut the book and poured himself a glass of water. "She was a good mother, she could drive anything with a steering wheel, she took good care of her family and she had a laugh that made everyone else laugh along with her."

The truth came through hard and clear. "And you were in love with her."

He gave her a steady look. "Since I was thirteen. My brother never knew, thank God. She loved him, not me, though it took me a long time to see it."

"Did she know?"

He shrugged. "Probably. Seems like women sense these things, but she never said anything, of course."

"I'm sorry."

"I didn't tell you so you'd be sorry."

She stood and walked over to him. "Then why? Because you wish I wasn't here?"

He lifted a strand of her hair from her shoulder and rubbed it between his thumb and index finger. "I don't know. You're doing everything but wearing her clothes, and I don't know how to act."

"What do you mean?"

"I mean," he whispered, dipping his head down lower, so his mouth was near her ear, "I don't know whether to make love to you or send you back to wherever you came from."

Sylvie shivered, more from the brush of his lips than his words. He wouldn't send her away—not with Christmas so close and the children so happy. He was a hard man, but he wasn't cruel. "You wouldn't do that."

"Wouldn't do what?" He cupped her chin when she would have moved away, but his fingers were gentle.

"Either one," she dared.

"Want to bet?" He brushed his lips across hers in a light motion that made her yearn for more. And then he kissed her. Really kissed her. As if he had to taste the feel of her mouth against his or go crazy with wanting. She didn't know how her arms ended up wrapped around his neck, or how his large hands encircled her waist and held her close against him—so close she could feel his arousal, so close she could feel the heat emanating from his body.

One of them came to their senses, but Sylvie couldn't remember exactly how they broke apart, or why. She only knew that she was cold and he was gone and she had to wrap her arms around herself to keep from shaking.

She'd never been kissed quite like that, Sylvie realized later on, when the dust had settled and she was back in her bedroom. She liked him— maybe too much—but despite everything, she had no business responding to him that way. He meant well, although this time of year seemed painful for him. But he loved those kids, and he took care of them. She couldn't compete with the ghost of Deb Brockett and she didn't want to. She had to remember that any feelings she had for Joe were only part of this holiday fantasy. Mom, Dad, kids, baby and Grandpa.

A lovely fantasy, but she was through with dreams. A long time ago she'd dreamed that someone would come along and adopt her. And then she'd dreamed of a home of her own with a man who loved her. She'd thought Billy Ray was the answer to her prayers. He was all smiles and charm and he didn't treat her as if she was invisible. He'd flirted, but in a nice way. And she'd gone along with it, even though she'd known he was a wandering rodeo rider. She'd thought he'd settle down.

Well, he hadn't. And a week from tomorrow she'd be back to dealing with the reality of single motherhood.

8

"TAKE SYLVIE WITH YOU," Hank said. "We need groceries and she might as well pick them out herself—you know, the way women like to do."

"But—" Joe began.

"I don't have to go. I can give Joe a list," Sylvie interrupted. She reached for the pad of paper by the phone. "Just give me a minute."

"Easier if you go yourself," Hank grumbled. "Will that boy of yours take a bottle?"

"He did once, but—"

"Then you fix one and leave it with me," Hank insisted. "We'll get along just fine, and that way you won't have to hurry back."

"I've never left Dillon before," Sylvie said, looking stricken.

Joe knew she didn't want to go to town with him—not after last night—but she couldn't tell Hank that. The old man was matchmaking again. Either that, or he was trying to be nice, giving her some time in town to get food. Giving her some time away from being a mother.

"Come to town," he said, hoping she would and praying she wouldn't. He didn't need the temptation of her sitting beside him in the truck;

didn't need to be breathing the same air or looking at something he couldn't—shouldn't—have.

Hank shook his head. "I've taken care of babies before, honey. And I'll sure take good care of this one." Sure enough, Dillon was tucked like a football against Hank's wide chest. The baby looked content and sleepy.

"I've only given him formula once. He made a face, but then he drank it."

She was starting to give in, Joe realized. How did the old man do it?

"Well, there you go," Hank said. "Nothing to worry about. We'll get along just fine."

Joe hesitated, his hand on the doorknob. "I'll warm up the Jeep. Just come out when you're ready." Which was about as gracious an invitation as she was likely to get, considering he didn't want to take her with him in the first place. He wasn't going to apologize for last night. He wasn't going to pretend it hadn't happened, either.

They were halfway to town before she spoke. She cleared her throat and half turned toward him. "Could we talk about Christmas?"

"Yeah," he said. How could a woman make one holiday so complicated? How could one woman make him think of stopping the truck and having sex with her on the front seat? "Are you warm enough?"

"Yes, I'm fine."

He adjusted the heat, then clamped both hands on the steering wheel and waited for her to talk about whatever was on her mind this time.

"Do you have presents for the kids?"

"Sure."

"Do you mind if I ask what you bought?" She pulled some papers out of her pocket. "They gave me lists for Santa. Of course, Karen doesn't believe in him, but Janie and Peter do."

"I ordered some god-awful baby doll for Janie from the catalog."

"What catalog?"

"Here." He pulled a wad of paper from his jacket pocket and tossed it over to her. "I got a notice from JCPenney saying this stuff was in and ready to be picked up."

She unfolded it and read it out loud. "'Micro Machine set, Lego rocket, sleeping bag, Drink Baby, CD player—'"

"For Karen."

"Who also wants a kitten."

"A what?"

"A *white* kitten, actually," Sylvie said, rustling through the papers on her lap. "From Buttrey's."

He couldn't help chuckling. "Last time I heard, they weren't selling cats at the grocery store."

"If I find one, can I get it for her?"

Joe shrugged. "I guess. Was there anything else she wanted? I thought I'd pick up a couple of CDs to go with the CD player."

"You can take her list."

He glanced at her again. Her cheeks were

pink and she looked very serious, as if the world was going to come to an end if the kids didn't get exactly what they wanted for Christmas. "You don't have to get so worked up over this. The kids will be happy no matter what," he assured her. "Christmas doesn't have to be perfect."

She turned those blue eyes upon him. "Oh, yes," she said, very serious. "It certainly does. I want to make sure that everything is just the way it should be. That's what Hank is paying me for." She found another piece of paper. "What do you usually have for Sunday dinner?"

"Whatever Hank feels like making, I guess."

"I thought about roast beef, but that's tricky. All that 'Medium or rare?' business, you know."

"Anything would—"

"I thought of chicken," she mused. "But chicken is too plain. What about a lasagna?"

Joe wisely decided not to come up with an opinion. "Just do what you want. It's no big deal, really."

"It *is* a big deal," she insisted. "Hank's trying to pretend it's not, but I can tell."

"What does Hank have to do with this?" He glanced over to see her frown.

"He didn't tell you?"

"No." Joe turned onto the main road and stepped on the accelerator. "Was he supposed to?"

"He's invited…someone to dinner Sunday afternoon."

"And?"

She didn't answer right away. "A lady friend."

"Hank doesn't have lady friends."

"He does now."

Joe glanced at her again. "Who?"

"Someone named Ruby. A hairdresser in town. Maybe I shouldn't have said anything."

"He couldn't keep it secret for long," Joe assured her, knowing that if the boisterous hairdresser was involved, everyone in town would know whom she went out with. "Not in Willum. Everyone here knows everyone else's business."

"If I wanted to find someone in town, who would I go to?"

"The café, I guess. Or the sheriff's office. Why?"

"It's not important." She riffled through the Christmas lists again. "So you think a lasagna would be a nice change for Sunday?"

"Hank bringing a date up to the ranch is a pretty big change all by itself." Joe couldn't quite figure that out. The old man never mentioned Ruby Dee, never talked about seeing anyone. Never talked about *wanting* to see anyone.

"Why? Is there something wrong?"

"I just didn't think he was interested in going out with anyone, that's all."

"He's a little nervous about it. Don't tell him I told you, okay?"

Joe slowed down and turned into town. Icy ruts lined the main street, and piles of snow bordered the sidewalks. "When was he figuring to tell me?"

"I don't know," Sylvie replied. "I guess he hadn't gotten up the courage yet."

Joe didn't know what courage had to do with anything. Either the man was still in mourning for his wife or he wasn't. And that was Hank's business, though Joe couldn't shake the feeling that somehow it just wasn't right. He and Hank were both "one woman" men. And when a man loved a woman, it should be for the rest of his life. "Do you have errands or do you want to go right to the grocery store?"

"I'd like to go to the bank," Sylvie said, sounding almost embarrassed. "Hank paid me yesterday, and I have some shopping to do, myself."

He parked the truck in front of the sporting-goods store and took the key out of the ignition before he turned to his passenger. "I'll meet you in Buttrey's in an hour and a half," he said, trying to act as if he escorted a woman to town every Friday. "Is that enough time?"

"It's perfect," she said, giving him one of those rare smiles that made him start to sweat. She gave him back his JCPenney's invoice. "Is there anything else you want me to get for the children?"

"No. Thanks." He watched her hop out of the truck and make her way carefully along the icy sidewalk. She paused in front of the window of Carol's Casuals, then walked purposefully toward the corner where the Willum County Bank had stood since 1907. Women sure liked to shop. Well, he hoped Sylvie would spend her money wisely. No matter how "perfect" Christmas became, Sylvie's job at the Rocky T wasn't going to last forever.

Before the end of the year, that woman was going to have to go back to wherever she came from.

"DO YOU THINK I SHOULD get a perm?" Karen put down her fork, pushed her empty plate aside and waited for her grandfather's guest to dispense beauty advice.

Sylvie almost laughed aloud at Joe's horrified expression. Karen might as well have asked if she could dye her hair purple. But if anyone could dispense beauty advice, it would the woman seated beside Hank at the kitchen table. Ruby Dee was a combination of Dinah Shore and Dolly Parton, a woman who was not afraid of eye shadow, mascara or jewelry. Sylvie figured she was the kind of woman anybody would want as her best friend or next-door neighbor. Ruby liked to laugh and she seemed to enjoy every bit of food that was put on her plate.

Sylvie and the Brockett children were fascinated, while Hank and Joe looked a little stunned. They probably hadn't had this much excitement on the ranch since that Blizzard of '48 Hank was always talking about.

"Well, honey," the hairdresser drawled, carefully considering the child, "I don't think you really need one. Your hair has a lot of body." She reached across the table and fingered a strand of

Karen's hair. "You have nice texture already. Besides, the teenagers aren't doing too many perms these days."

Karen didn't look convinced. "What about being blond? You know, streaks? Like the girls on *Baywatch?*"

"*Baywatch?*" Hank echoed. "When have you seen a show like that?"

"At my friend's house." Karen focused her attention on her grandfather's company.

"Does everyone want coffee with dessert?" Sylvie stood and began clearing the plates.

"I do," Joe said, pushing back his chair. He picked up his plate and Peter's, who sat to his right. "Uh, Mrs. Dee, do you want tea or coffee?"

"Coffee would be just fine, but I told you to call me Ruby, now didn't I? I went back to my maiden name after two divorces, so don't go calling me 'Mrs.' anything because it brings back bad memories." She smiled at Joe and ruffled Janie's golden curls. "Now, here's someone who won't ever need to spend her hard-earned money on a perm at the Hair Hut."

"What's a perm?"

"Sex," her brother told her.

Hank tipped over his water glass. *"Sex?"* He looked around the table as Ruby reached over and calmly dabbed at the spill with her napkin. "What kind of shows are you kids watching over here? I should never have gotten that damn satellite dish."

"I love my dish," Ruby said. "I learned some

of those new line dances on the country-western channel." She dangled a wrist coated with silver bracelets toward Sylvie. "See these, honey? All from the shopping network. On sale, too." She shook her finger at Peter. "And a *perm*, young man, is different from, well, what you thought. A perm is what ladies do to get their hair made all curly."

"Like yours?"

"Exactly. Aren't you smart!"

"Probably from those TV shows," Hank grumbled.

Sylvie turned toward Joe and smiled. He grinned back and shook his head as if to say he couldn't quite believe what an odd Sunday afternoon this had been. She was surprised he was helping her clear the table. He even went back to the counter and started pouring coffee into the good china cups while Sylvie placed thick squares of cranberry cake on dessert plates and ladled warm butter sauce over each serving.

He stepped closer to her and whispered, "I'll bet that 'sperm' story is told at the Hair Hut tomorrow morning."

"They're closed on Mondays," Sylvie said. She'd looked at the hours painted on the door Friday. Just in case she ever decided to get her hair done. Not that she should spend money in such a frivolous way, but sometimes it was tempting to dream of looking pretty. Maybe Joe wouldn't glare at her so often if she looked less like a homeless stray and more confident, more like Ruby Dee.

"What's going on here?" he asked, still standing close. She could smell the pleasant trace of aftershave and for one insane second was tempted to lean her cheek against his shoulder. She had washed and folded that blue flannel shirt yesterday and she knew it would be soft against her skin.

She continued to fix the desserts until all seven were ready. "What do you mean?"

"Hank and Ruby."

She picked up two plates and forced Joe to move aside so she could pass. His thigh brushed hers, but she told herself that she didn't feel a thing. "I guess you'll have to ask him," she said, keeping her voice low. "Maybe he's lonely."

"Maybe we all are," he answered, his voice sounding almost sad.

"What do you mean?" She looked up at him, but he avoided meeting her gaze and didn't reply. Instead he picked up two of the plates and followed her to the table.

Sylvie served Ruby first, then Hank. She kept busy refilling coffee cups and replenishing paper napkins. When everyone had finished dessert, Sylvie refused all offers of help. Dillon was still asleep and she didn't mind having the kitchen to herself. She would scrub and rinse and dry and wipe and keep so busy she wouldn't remember the times Joe smiled at her. Or how nice he'd been in town Friday. Or on Saturday, when he'd been out working all day and didn't frown at her when he walked into the kitchen for supper.

"Come see my tree," Janie told Ruby. "Santa's gonna love it."

"I'll just bet he will, honey," the older woman agreed. "But you all go on now. I'm going to help your—Sylvie with the dishes." The child ran off to join the others that Ruby had shooed into the living room, and Ruby turned to Sylvie. "I almost called you her mother," she said. "You're so good with those children, a person would think you'd always been here."

Sylvie continued rinsing the plates. "Sometimes I have to remind myself that I'm not their mother, that I'm not Deb Brockett. But being housekeeper here is an easy job. They're good kids."

"I could tell." Ruby moved glasses and silverware from the table until all that was left was the stained white linen cloth. "Why don't you let me wash up those pots?"

"No way. I get paid for this. You don't." She shut the dishwasher door and flipped the handle to the On position. "All I have to do is wash up what's left in the sink."

Ruby reached over and plucked the sponge from the dishpan. "Then I'll make myself useful by wiping off the counters."

"You really don't—"

"I *want* to," Ruby declared. "I miss that cleaning-up-the-kitchen girl talk." She winked. "You never know what you'll hear when women get together in the kitchen."

"Or at the hairdresser's?"

"That's right. I think I know everyone's secrets."

"Really?"

"Yes, honey, but I keep the scissors moving and my mouth shut. It's a small town. Why, when that ad for a wife went up in town you should have heard—" Ruby stopped and shot Sylvie an apologetic smile. "Sorry. I shouldn't have brought that up. I forgot—"

"It's okay. I'm long past being embarrassed." She started rinsing the pots and setting them on the drainer.

Ruby found a dish towel and, bracelets jangling, began to dry them. "Well, I wouldn't be embarrassed about wanting to marry that Joe Brockett. There're more than a few women in town who wouldn't mind *that* job."

"Does he go out with any of them?"

"Not too many that I've heard about, and believe me, I'd hear if there was anything going on." She chuckled. "Besides, from the way he looks at you, I figure those other women don't have a chance."

Sylvie felt her face turn hot. "Do people think we're, uh, sleeping together?"

"Honey, people will think anything they want to think. All I'm saying is, that man looks at you like he's winter and you're spring and it's time for flowers to bloom and birds to sing."

"Ruby, I don't—"

"No." The bracelets jangled again as Ruby wagged her index finger. "You listen to me. I haven't always had the best luck with men, but I sure know people." A sad expression clouded her blue eyes. "And I've made some mistakes, too. But," she cautioned, "I know that when a man looks at a woman like that man looks at you, well, something is going to happen."

"I've had enough things happening in my life," Sylvie said. "Now I have a baby. And not much else."

Ruby nodded. "I've been there, honey, and it's not an easy road. But all you can do is your best."

"You have children, Ruby?"

"Yes, and he was a handful. And still is," she admitted, picking up a saucepan and giving it a swipe with the towel. "What's your boy's name?"

"Dillon."

"After the folk singer?"

"After the town." She rinsed the last pot and handed it to Ruby to dry, then pulled the plug from the drain. "I'd better go up and check on him. It's about time for him to wake up and start crying."

"You go on," Ruby said, wiping the pot quickly. "But Sylvie?"

She turned. "Yes?"

"I know it's none of my business, but you seem like a sweet girl." She lowered her voice to a whisper. "I've seen your face when you look at that man, too. And I'm going to guess you're halfway in love with Joe. Be careful, honey. He's looking at you like he wants you for dessert, but that doesn't mean you'll be walking down the aisle. Joe Brockett's thirty-five and still single, and he's real good at staying that way."

"I'm not looking to get married, Ruby." *Not anymore.* "All *I* want for Christmas is a place to call home, just so I can tell my son about his first Christmas and how wonderful it was."

"All right," Ruby agreed, wiping a touch of moisture from under her eyes. "I'll mind my own business, but if you ever need a friend or—" she smiled "—a shampoo and cut, you know who to come to."

"Thanks, Ruby." Sylvie impulsively leaned over and kissed the woman's cheek. "You might just see me at the Hair Hut one of these days."

"Miz Ruby!" Janie ran into the kitchen. "Are you coming? Grandpa put the lights on. Do you know what I'm asking Santa for?"

Ruby put out her hand and the little girl took it and tugged her toward the door. "I just couldn't even begin to guess, honey. You'll have to tell me everything."

Sylvie followed them into the hall, but went upstairs instead of going into the living room. She opened the bedroom door in time to hear Dillon let out his first complaining "Hey, I'm awake" wail. She soothed him, changed his diaper and then, propped up against the bed's headboard, she nursed him and thought about what Ruby had said.

He looks at you like he's winter and you're spring and it's time for flowers to bloom....

Sylvie leaned back and closed her eyes. She didn't want to remember the two times that Joe had kissed her, but she couldn't forget those kisses, either. And she wouldn't make the mistake of thinking they meant anything, even if they had turned her heart upside down and backward.

Ruby had a way with words.

And Ruby had warned her.

"YOU GO FIX YOURSELF a stiff drink, son." Hank grabbed his hat and jammed it on his head. "I'm not gonna stay here and argue with you tonight, dammit. You go drown your sorrows in a bottle, if that's what you want to do. I'm going home to bed."

"Hank—"

"Hell, Joe," the old man grumbled. "Today was *good*. We haven't had that much fun since, well, Jim and Deb were here. You have to admit that Ruby and Sylvie and all that Christmas stuff sure livens things up."

"Ruby, maybe," Joe admitted, turning his back on the festive Christmas tree. He didn't want to argue with his old friend, but he didn't understand what was happening, either. He wanted things back the way they were—when he didn't know there was a woman named Sylvie Smith in the world; when he didn't walk around wanting to take her to bed for an hour or two, just to get it out of his system. "Hell, Hank, we've been doing okay by ourselves."

"Yeah?" He shook his head. "Well, 'okay' isn't enough for me. I've got a few good years left and I wouldn't mind having some female company once in a while. And I'd suggest the same for you, before you get any grumpier."

"I'm not grumpy."

Hank snorted. "The hell you're not. You're a miserable pain in the ass most of the time. That little gal has you tied up in knots and you're not man enough to admit it."

"I'm not going to admit what isn't true." He followed Hank into the kitchen. "Don't go, Hank. It's not even nine o'clock yet. We can play a couple of hands of gin rummy or something."

"It's late enough for me." Hank pulled his gloves from his jacket pocket and opened the back door. "You'll have to find something else to do besides play cards."

Hank didn't even look back. Joe stood in the dark kitchen and listened to the silence. The kids were asleep. Sylvie had gone upstairs with the baby an hour ago and hadn't ever come back down. He supposed she was tired out from all that cooking, but he wouldn't have minded some company.

Anything would be better than being alone with his own thoughts.

He poured himself a glass of bourbon and took his drink into the living room, where the only light came from the multicolored bulbs on the ridiculous tree. He took a sip of his drink and turned his back on the decorations. He'd had enough of Christmas talk, enough of what the kids wanted from Santa.

No one asked me what I want.

"What?"

Joe jumped, almost spilling his drink, when he heard Sylvie's voice. "Hell!"

She took a few steps into the room. Her hair was mussed and her cheeks flushed, as if she'd just awakened from a nap. "Who were you talking to?"

"Myself, I guess," he admitted. Which meant he was in worse shape than he'd thought. "I guess I was thinking out loud."

She smiled, but she didn't come any closer. He noticed her feet were bare, though she still wore those faded jeans and that damn blue sweater. She had tiny toes, and for one insane moment he wondered what those little feet would feel like if her legs were wrapped around his.

"What *do* you want?" She tilted her head slightly, as if the question was as serious as the price of hay. "The children would like some ideas."

"The children wouldn't be able to give me what I want," he replied, keeping his gaze on her face. She understood what he was talking about, all right, but to her credit she didn't run screaming up the stairs.

"What makes you think I would?"

The curiosity in her voice surprised him. "I've kissed you a few times, remember?"

"Twice," she corrected. "And that doesn't mean I'm...going to bed with you."

He set his empty glass on the table and stood to face her. "It doesn't?" She didn't answer, but he didn't expect her to. "In all this holiday foolishness, with all the lists and all the preparations, you haven't asked me what *I* want, Sylvie. It's not a pony or creamed onions or a kitten, either."

"No?"

He could have sworn she smiled, but he figured he must have imagined it. He stepped closer, ran his finger down the line of her cheek, to one corner of that perfect mouth. "No," he said, his voice husky with need.

"Maybe you'd better make a list," she said, and her lips trembled under his finger.

He was tired of pretending he didn't want her. He was even tired of wanting her, he figured, and there was only one way to take care of it, once and for all. "Maybe I'd better take you to bed instead."

9

"MAYBE YOU SHOULD," Sylvie heard herself reply. When had she become so brave? Or was this the foolish behavior of a woman tired of being alone?

"My bed or yours?" He gazed at her with those dark eyes as if daring her to change her mind.

"Yours, of course."

His hand cupped her chin and lifted it slightly. "'Of course'?"

"Dillon is sleeping."

"Of course." He touched his lips to hers as if testing to see if she would stay or run, then asked, "How much time do we have before he wakes?"

"An hour," she managed, because his hand had dipped under the hem of her sweater to stroke her waist. "Or two." His hand roamed higher and cupped her breast. "Maybe, uh, three."

"You're so very soft," he said, smoothing his palm along her skin. "I thought you would be."

"It's baby powder. I had a shower and—"

He took her lips again—a tender kiss that made her catch her breath with the wonder of it all. She was in his arms, pressed against that wide warm chest, for all the world as if she was someone he loved. No, she told herself, her hands clinging to his shoulders, she wouldn't think of love. Love would spoil everything.

She parted her lips and his tongue entered her slowly, as if he was making love to her with his mouth. His hands stopped at her waist, holding her still so he could taste her. He withdrew slightly and Sylvie followed, wanting more, needing to make love to him as he made love to her.

"Put your arms around my neck," he said, scooping her into his arms as if she weighed less than a baby calf. Sylvie knew she could stop this, knew that with one word he would put her back on her feet to go to bed alone. Instead she found the soft skin of his neck, just above his collar, and tasted that warmth with delicate kisses.

He carried her up the dark staircase and into his bedroom, a room that she had only peered into once and decided against cleaning. Sylvie could see the dark shadow of the double bed, the only light coming from the window where outside snow reflected the half-moon's glow. Joe placed her on the bed and locked the bedroom door.

"I never pictured you here, waiting for me in my bed," he said before sitting beside her. The mattress dipped under his weight and tilted her toward him.

"Neither did I." She didn't want to think about what she was doing. She didn't want to think about the morning, or the day after that, or Christmas or presents or what she would serve for dinner. It had been a long time since she had been held.

It had been a long time since she had felt as if she wasn't alone.

He kissed her, which—oddly—made everything all right—even though it made no sense to be here, being lowered onto the bed of the man who didn't want or need a woman in his life.

But Sylvie didn't want to be anywhere else. She loved the feel of his rough-skinned hands on her body. When he eased the hem of her sweater high, over her breasts, Sylvie removed her warmest piece of clothing and tossed it to the floor. She reached for his shirt and, one by one, unfastened the buttons until that hard, furred chest was exposed to her fingertips. Somehow they managed to get the rest of their clothes off and lay bare every inch of skin to kisses and touching. He was gentle with her sensitive breasts, tender with her body newly healed from giving birth.

He touched her until she was wet and open, until she reached for him and said only, "Now," and Joe reached into the nightstand drawer and retrieved a condom.

Sylvie held her breath as he began to enter her, then exhaled slowly as he slid inside and almost out again.

"All right?" he asked, leaning over her to take her lips once more. She urged him closer. And deeper. Until the whirl of sensation took her to a place where everything centered on his body in-side hers. A place where she couldn't think past a brief amazement that anything could feel this good. When he slipped his hands underneath her buttocks and pulled her closer against him, she was lost. She peaked and shattered into a million starry pieces and Joe moaned against her mouth and found his own release. He kissed her until they could find their breath; kissed her un-til there was nothing to say, even if either one of them knew what words would make sense.

He rolled off her gently and tucked her against his shoulder. She closed her eyes and felt him move the sheet across her bare shoulder be-fore he left the bed.

Sylvie slept for a while—a dreamless con-tented hour of rest. She woke with a start and felt the unfamiliar warmth of a man's body next to hers. She turned carefully, only to see him open his eyes. Joe, with an intense expression on his face, propped himself up on an elbow and gazed down at her.

"Who was he?"

Sylvie blinked. "You think you have the right to ask me questions like that now?"

"I'm not talking about 'rights,'" Joe said. "I'm asking, who was the son of a bitch who left you to raise his son all by yourself?"

"It doesn't matter anymore," she lied, turning away. She wished she weren't naked. She wished she didn't have to fumble around to find her clothes while Joe watched.

"But you came to town to find him."

She didn't answer. She was too busy tugging her sweater over her head.

"And," he continued, "he wasn't here."

"Gee, you're really smart, you know that?"

"Sarcasm isn't your style, Sylvie."

She stopped, hugging the rest of her clothes to her waist to cover her nakedness, and looked at his outline in the darkness. "You'd rather talk to the quiet, pathetic little homeless woman who bakes cinnamon rolls and owns only one pair of jeans, wouldn't you?" She started toward the door. "Well, you didn't make love to that woman, *Mr. Brockett.* You just had sex—pretty good sex, too, I figure, from the happy look on your face." Her bra dropped and she scooped it from the floor before continuing. "You just *had sex* with someone who doesn't think that owning a ranch and having money in the bank gives you the right to act all high-and-mighty."

"Sylvie—"

She struggled to figure out how to unlock the door. "Damn it, let me out of here!"

He gently wrapped his arms around her. "Don't go. I'll apologize."

She kept her hand on the doorknob and tried to ignore the enticing feel of his naked body against hers.

He kissed the back of her neck. "I'm tired of that sweater. Could you take it off again? Please?"

She sighed. "I'm not finished yelling at you."

"I said I was sorry." His hands found her breasts and soon the bundle of clothes lay on the floor, along with the sweater. She turned in his arms, her skin to his, his heart pounding against her cheek as he held her with her back against the door. "I *don't* think of you as some homeless pathetic person. Not in the last few days, anyway."

"I don't like to think of myself that way, either," she said.

He leaned closer, surrounding her with his warmth. "Let me make love to you again."

"Dillon could wake up soon." It was a feeble excuse. And she really didn't want to leave. Not yet.

"We'll hear him if he cries." He smiled. "Believe me, we'll hear him. That kid of yours has a set of lungs that could spook a herd of cattle into Idaho."

He was hard against her thigh, so she relaxed against the wall and let him lean into her as he bent down to kiss her. She opened her legs, enough to let him move between her thighs. She was suddenly slick and warm and ready for him, but though he lifted her from the waist and fitted her against him, he didn't enter her.

"I'm going to carry you over to the bed," he murmured against her hair. "For God's sake, don't kick me."

She wriggled, just to tease him, but in one short minute their problems were solved and she was in his lap. This time he lifted her above him and she slid onto him as she braced her knees on either side of his thighs and wrapped her arms around his neck.

It was a long time before either one slept.

OH, CHRIST, WHAT HAD HE done? He smelled like sex; the bed smelled like sex. The whole damn room smelled like a bordello and he was as drained as if he'd spent the night with the naked triplets that graced the cover of the girlie magazine in Hawkins's gas station. Not that he'd ever fantasized about making it with three big-busted blondes—at least not since he'd been a teenager—but Joe now could guess how a man would feel if he'd actually survived until daybreak.

He needed a shower. He needed a couple of aspirin. And he needed to have his brain examined to see if there was any common sense left.

Because he'd sure lost any sense he might have had the minute he'd thought about what he *really* wanted for Christmas and had hauled his housekeeper upstairs.

Joe sat up and swung his legs over the side of the bed and started cursing himself. He had made love with Sylvie. Not once. Not twice. But three times—the last one especially sweet and slow in the warm cocoon of blankets as the north wind blasted against the second story of the old house.

And then…the baby had cried. Howled, actually, in that spine-shattering way he had of announcing his hunger in the middle of the night. Sylvie had untangled herself and, dragging clothes and scooping up underwear, taken off like a rocket. She was out of his room and back where she belonged in a matter of seconds.

Leaving Joe to pass out in the quiet that arrived the minute Dillon discovered his meal ticket. Now, with morning light filtering through Deb's homemade curtains, he felt about as close to death as a man could be without actually calling for an ambulance.

And if Hank discovered what had gone on here half the night, Joe was a dead man, anyway. What the hell had possessed him? If he'd only tried harder, he could have survived without sex awhile longer.

SYLVIE TRIED NOT TO burst into a chorus of "Frosty the Snowman." She couldn't hold a tune and really hoped Dillon hadn't inherited her tendency to sing off-key, but she was happy. Happy for the first time in many months.

She was the first one into the kitchen, which was unusual, since normally Joe was awake before the first light. She'd made the coffee and whipped up a bowl of pancake batter. The eggs were beaten and ready to be scrambled in the buttered skillet when she heard his footsteps on the stairs. She promised herself she wouldn't blush when he walked into the kitchen. She was ready with a smile.

He didn't look at her.

"Good morning," she said, waiting for a smile or a look or a kiss.

"Is the coffee ready?" he asked, as if he didn't have fresh coffee waiting for him every morning. Every night before she went to bed she fixed the pot and set the automatic timer to come on at four forty-five.

"Help yourself." He didn't meet her gaze, so Sylvie turned back to the stove and fumbled with the skillets until she could compose herself. She heard him open the cupboard and pour the coffee. She listened as he pulled out a chair and sat down in his usual place.

She fixed his breakfast and wondered if he felt as shy as she did. When she placed his plate of pancakes and eggs in front of him, she waited for a smile. Or a look. Something that said, *Last night was incredible.*

"Can I have a fork?"

"A fork," she repeated, putting her hands on her hips.

"And some more butter, too," he said, pushing the empty dish toward her. He avoided looking at her. "We're out."

"Sure." She opened the fridge and got out another stick of butter. She peeled the wrapper off it and dumped it into the dish by Joe's knuckles, then she got a fork out of the drawer and tossed it on the table beside his coffee mug. "Just tell me this, Mr. Brockett."

This time he looked up. Briefly. "What?"

"Did we sleep together last night or did I just dream the fact that you carried me upstairs and took off all my clothes and told me what you wanted Mrs. Santa to do to you?"

"Jeez, Sylvie." He looked past her as if expecting the entire town of Willum to be standing there listening to their conversation. Then he frowned at her. "Keep your voice down."

"Never mind." She sighed. "I know the answer. Last night never happened. I understand." Sylvie returned to the stove and her own lukewarm cup of coffee. She took a sip and pretended to look through a holiday cookbook while Joe finished his breakfast.

He brought his dirty plate and silverware to the sink. "I'm sorry, Sylvie. Last night shouldn't have happened."

"I guess you're right," she said, flipping another page and staring at a photo of a tree-shaped coffee cake.

"It won't happen again," he promised.

"No," she said, picking up her coffee cup with a hand she was proud to see didn't shake. "Of course it won't."

"WHERE'D SHE GO?"

Joe pushed the plate of leftover pie closer to Hank. "Help yourself."

"Thanks. Where is she?"

"She headed to town. Said she had some last-minute shopping to do, since tomorrow's Christmas Eve." Joe didn't believe her—not really. He figured she wanted to get away for a while. Away from him and away from any embarrassment about last night.

"Well, that doesn't make any sense," Hank grumbled, digging another helping from the pie plate. "She was just there on Saturday and I told her if she needed anything else I'd be glad to go to town and get it for her."

Joe shrugged. "You know women. They like to shop for themselves."

"And the baby?

"She took him with her, said she had some kind of backpack to carry him in."

"You look tired, Joe. You sleepin' okay? Maybe you'd better not ride out this afternoon, or at least not all the way to the south pasture."

"She said she'd pick up Janie at the preschool before she came home. I guess there was going to be a party." He stood and looked out the window. "You think it's going to storm?"

"Nope."

"You sure? I don't like the looks of that sky." And Sylvie had taken that little car of hers instead of the Jeep. He should have argued about that, but he'd been too busy trying not to look at her. Looking at her just made him remember last night, and remembering last night made him hard all over again.

"Do you think I'm too old?"

Joe turned back to Hank. "For what?"

"For Ruby."

So that was why Hank was grumpy. "I guess you'd have to ask *her* that."

"She might not tell me the truth."

"Why not?"

"So she wouldn't hurt my feelings. If she did think I was too old for her."

Joe went over to the counter and poured himself his thirtieth cup of coffee. At this rate he was going to stay awake till New Year's. "She laughed at your jokes."

"That's a good sign."

"And she didn't seem in a big hurry to leave—until it started getting dark."

Hank cleared his throat. "She asked me to stop by her place the next time I was in town."

"You going to do it?"

"I don't know. If I poke my nose into the Hair Hut, it'll be all over town that I've got myself a girlfriend." He sighed. "But I guess I'm ready for a little female companionship." He gave Joe a sharp look. "And from the looks of you, I'd say so are you."

"I'm fine, Hank. I'm fine just the way I am." Joe wished he'd sounded more convincing—especially when Hank leaned back in his chair and laughed.

SYLVIE SPENT ELEVEN dollars of her dwindling cash on one of those disposable cameras, a box of candy canes, and assorted small gifts for the Brockett children. Dillon wouldn't remember his first Christmas, but someday he would be able to look at the pictures and see a real family.

For now, her son slept against her chest, secure and warm in the little carrier she'd bought at a secondhand store before he was born. She'd nursed him at the most private place she could find in town: the library. No one had paid any attention to a woman sitting facing the corner grouping of poetry books, a shopping bag filled with gifts by her side on the floor.

In the freezer at the ranch were a foil-wrapped package of cinnamon buns for Hank to enjoy after she was gone and thick oatmeal raisin cookies for Joe to take with him when he went on those long trips to check on the cattle.

There was only one thing left, and that was risky and complicated and ridiculous. But she owed it to Karen to try, at least. The child had given her and Dillon a home for Christmas and Sylvie owed her something special. If the notice was still at Buttrey's and if there were any left, Karen would have *one* wish come true on Christmas morning.

Willum was crowded with last-minute shoppers, so Sylvie left her car parked on Main Street, in front of the women's clothing store with the windows decorated with silver snowflakes and artificial snow. Thick silver necklaces draped over turtleneck sweaters paired with expensive-looking slacks and colorful socks. Next door was a gift shop, its windows filled with ceramic houses that were lit with tiny bulbs and grouped together to form a village, complete with an ice-skating rink and tiny villagers going about their business.

Sylvie didn't linger long, especially since the wind had come up. She had an hour before picking up Janie, but if she had extra time she could sit in the café and sip hot chocolate and thaw out her chilled toes while Dillon lay warm and sleepy beside her on the booth's vinyl-coated bench.

Sylvie kept her head down until she'd

rounded the corner and the bank buffered the brunt of the wind. She waited for a moment while a pickup truck and an oversize station wagon stopped to let her cross the street. When she stepped up on the sidewalk, she saw the one person she thought she'd never see again.

Billy Ray Diamond, long and lean and laughing, stood pumping gas into a new red truck. His denim jacket flapped open and no hat covered his dark hair, which was longer than the last time she'd seen him. He'd never felt the cold, she remembered. And he was here, in Willum, Montana—a place he'd once referred to as "home."

Where he'd said they'd get married someday, as soon as he won a few fat purses on the rodeo circuit. As soon as he saved some money and paid back a few friends.

Sylvie didn't know why her steps slowed. She didn't know why she didn't hurry across the oily pavement of Hawkins Gas-to-Go and throw herself against the man she thought she loved more than life. Instead, she took a deep breath of frigid air and wrapped one arm around the little bundle of baby attached to her chest. She felt a little queasy, as if she'd drunk too much strong coffee on an empty stomach. Her heart was racing double time as she walked across the pavement toward the red pickup and Dillon's father.

"The son of a bitch who left you to raise his son all by yourself." Joe's words echoed through her head, but she didn't want to think about Joe, or about what had happened between them last

night. She had found Dillon's father. Maybe he had come looking for her, or maybe he'd gotten her last letters and followed her here.

"Billy Ray!" she called, but he had leaned into the open window of the truck to talk to someone in the driver's seat. She couldn't hurry—not with one hand holding her coat closed over Dillon and the other gripping plastic shopping bags. "Billy Ray!"

He still didn't hear her. Sylvie watched as he turned to hand money to a man in mechanic's overalls. She hurried as quickly as she could, and before Billy Ray could open the truck door, she was close enough to call his name again. He turned and stared.

She felt a relief so profound she almost sank into his arms. "You got my letters," she managed to say, though for some reason she was out of breath.

He dropped his gaze and opened the passenger-side door as if she hadn't said a word. She was close to the truck now, close enough to see the young blond woman behind the wheel. Close enough to see a fur-trimmed hood framing the face of a teenage beauty who gave her a bored look and started the engine.

Billy Ray disappeared into the truck and slammed the door. He shot one horrified look at his son and turned away, as if he was busy telling his new sweetheart that there must be some mistake.

Sylvie could only imagine what excuses he'd

make. She'd heard enough of them in the two years they were together.

"Ma'am?" The mechanic came out, wiping his hands on a greasy rag. "You okay?"

"I'm fine," she lied. She'd expected Billy Ray would feel something when he saw his own son. She'd thought he had a heart, but she'd been mistaken. "Who was that woman in the red truck?"

"Cissy Boyle. Her daddy owns one of the biggest cattle ranches in the valley." He shook his head. "She's hell on wheels, that one is. She's a barrel racer, too. On the rodeo circuit now with her new husband. Do you know them?"

"No." She watched as the truck turned down Main Street and sped off. She shivered as a gust of wind blew her hair across her face. "I thought I did, but I was wrong."

10

SYLVIE WASN'T GOING TO let a little thing like rejection ruin her Christmas. She continued walking to Buttrey's, wrote down the phone number of the ad on the bulletin board, found a pay phone in the corner near the frozen foods, and even had three swallows of free coffee at the front of the store. Dillon slept, content and warm, unaware that his father had been so close.

Unaware that his father hadn't wanted to acknowledge either one of them.

She knew now that she was better off without him. Better off without that kind of man raising her son. She'd been foolish to think otherwise, but she'd made some mistakes and she wasn't proud of any of them. Still, she'd done her best to find her son's father, to give Dillon a chance for some family. If anyone respected family, it was Sylvie Smith. Being raised an orphan made a person appreciate the idea of having a family. She'd dreamed of a loving home, children, a man who adored her. She'd dreamed of family reunions and holidays full of laughter. She'd wanted all that for herself, but she'd wanted it even more for her son. And she'd been a fool to think it could happen.

She didn't know where she'd gone wrong. It wasn't as if there was a long line of men in her past. She'd been in love with Billy Ray—or at least she'd sure thought she was—and like a fool she hadn't wanted to see the truth: that the man never intended to settle down or raise a son. If she'd been smarter, she would have seen that.

So by the time she had finished her errands, put her purchases carefully in the back of the car and headed for the Rocky T, Sylvie had made some decisions. She didn't know if the cold Montana air had cleared her head or if she'd finally grown up and faced reality, but she knew that if—and that was a pretty big if—she ever fell in love again, next time she would do it with her eyes wide open. Men were trouble, and she had no sense at all where they were concerned.

She would do her job, celebrate the holiday, make the most of having a pretend family for three more days. The road to the Rocky T led home. But only temporarily.

"IT'S HERE, IT'S REALLY here!" Karen shouted, twirling herself around the room. "Christmas Eve is here!"

"Don't get dizzy and crash into the tree," Uncle Joe warned. "Keep your eyes open."

"I will," she promised, loving the way the colored lights danced when she spun. "I'm too happy to sit still."

"Try anyway," Grandpa said. "You're gonna get Janie and Peter all wound up."

She collapsed on the couch and panted. "Too

late. Janie ate too many cookies and has a stomachache and Peter's making another list for Santa."

"That boy sure wants a lot of stuff." Grandpa folded the newspaper and tucked it into the magazine rack. "I suppose I'd better build a nice fire so you all can hang your stockings."

"No, Grandpa!" Janie shrieked. She ran into the room, tripped on the hem of her new pink nightgown and fell headlong into her uncle's arms. "Santa has to come down the chimney," she sputtered.

"Whoa," Uncle Joe warned, setting Janie on her feet. "You're going to get hurt if you don't stop running around. How's your stomachache?"

"Fine." She wriggled out of his grasp and climbed up on Grandpa's lap, so Karen hurried over to the big chair, too. She hoped Grandpa wouldn't tease too much and make Janie hyper. Then she'd never get to sleep, and Karen wanted their bedroom to be quiet, so the night would go by fast. She *thought* she'd heard Grandpa and Sylvie talking about a kitten before supper, but when she came into the kitchen they were talking about mittens. But they couldn't fool her. There was a kitten somewhere on the Rocky T, and it was going to be hers. And she would open her eyes wide and act very surprised when she saw it, so Sylvie's and Grandpa's feelings wouldn't be hurt because she'd guessed the secret.

Sylvie came into the living room with Dillon

in her arms. The baby was awake, his fat cheeks all pink and cute. He wore a little red sleeper and a red Santa hat with a white pompom dangling from the tip. Sylvie's hair was tied back with red Christmas ribbon and she wore her soft blue sweater, the one that smelled like baby powder and cinnamon.

Karen snuggled beside her on the couch, while Janie giggled in Grandpa's arms and Peter played trucks beneath the tree.

This was her lucky Christmas, Karen knew. With an almost-mom. And a sweet little baby. And cookies with green sugar and silver balls, just like her first mother made. This year there were packages under the tree that had candy canes tied with the red bows. There was going to be a fancy dinner, with the cloth table cover and white napkins that she'd helped Sylvie iron this afternoon. Nothing could go wrong. Not now.

Karen looked over at her uncle and frowned. If he'd only act nicer to Sylvie, then all of them could keep her forever. So she asked him a question that might make him look happy.

"Uncle Joe, what do *you* want for Christmas?"

His mouth dropped open but he didn't say anything. Weird. Uncle Joe usually had something to say if you asked him.

Sylvie cleared her throat. "I think Uncle Joe already got his present," she said, fixing Dillon's little hat so it wouldn't fall off. "Didn't you, Uncle Joe?"

"Uh, well," he stammered. "I guess so."

Karen smelled a rat. "What was it? A new saddle?"

"Not exactly."

"A pony?" Janie asked.

Grandpa was giving Uncle Joe a funny look. "You know you're not supposed to buy yourself anything ahead of time cuz it might spoil someone's surprise."

"It won't spoil anything," he said. Uncle Joe looked at Sylvie like he wished she hadn't talked about his present and Sylvie went back to playing with Dillon as if she didn't notice anything wrong at all.

"Well," Karen asked again, "what *did* you wish for?"

He winked at her. "I wished...that the Christmas tree would stop smelling like a pig barn."

Janie giggled while Uncle Joe leaned forward and pretended to sniff the tree. "Yep," he said. "Got my wish. All I can smell now is pine."

Karen sighed and leaned her head against Sylvie's shoulder. If Sylvie was going to like him, even a little bit, Uncle Joe was going to have to get a *whole* lot nicer, and right now that didn't seem real possible.

"WHO WANTS HOT chocolate?"

They all said yes, even Joe, who hadn't said two words to Sylvie since yesterday, when he'd said, *"It won't happen again."*

She'd wanted to tell him that for her it was more than sex. If she wasn't smarter now than she'd been forty-eight hours ago, she might have said that making love with him had been like being in love. She might even have thought that she was falling in love with him—just a little—and that it had made the night they'd spent together magic.

But she was wiser now. Too wise to fall in love—or to think about falling in love—after one night. Yesterday she'd realized she'd chased across two states looking for a worthless rodeo rider who'd conned her into believing his sweet love-talk while he'd been taking off her clothes.

Sylvie gave the baby to Karen to hold, who looked as if she was going to faint dead away from excitement. Well, Christmas was for kids, they said. Before she went into the kitchen, Sylvie grabbed her camera and took a picture of that happy scene. Then Janie and Peter gathered around and all four children had their picture taken under Deb Brockett's calico wreath.

"That's real nice," Hank said. "There's gonna be a real good memory in that picture."

"I could use a few of those," Sylvie said, softening her words with a smile for the old rancher.

"We'll make a few more, honey," Hank promised, plucking the camera from her hand. "Now stand over there beside Joe and smile real pretty."

She had no choice but to do as she was told and stood awkwardly between the tree and Joe.

"Stand up, Joe." Hank pointed toward the tree. "Stand over there beside Sylvie so I can get you both in front of the decorations."

Her shoulder touched his arm, his hand

brushed her thigh, and neither one moved to break the contact.

Later, as she heated the milk and stirred in chocolate-flavored powder, she remembered the brief touch of his arm against her. He had felt warm and solid. She might have imagined how he stood closer to her than he had to for the sake of a good photograph, but she hadn't imagined what had happened on Sunday night.

Now all she had to do was stop remembering.

JOE CHOSE TO READ "The Night before Christmas." It just seemed right, he decided, picking up the worn book that had belonged to his brother for so many years.

"I love this story," Janie declared, climbing into his lap.

"Speak right up," Hank said, draining the last of the hot chocolate from his cup. "And don't rush through it."

"I'm not going to rush." Joe waited for Sylvie to quit clearing cups and plates like she was some damn maid. "Sylvie," he said, sounding harsher than he meant to. "Sit down and stop fussing."

"I'm just going to take these to—"

"Do it later," Joe snapped, wanting her near him.

Karen glared at him, Peter stared and even Dillon let out a small cry.

"Please," Joe added, gesturing toward the empty space on the couch. "You want to hear 'The Night before Christmas,' don't you? I don't read it as well as my brother used to, but I'll give it my best shot."

Karen brightened. "I remember Daddy reading it to me."

Joe couldn't swallow the lump in his throat. "I do, too, honey. He read it every Christmas Eve, just like our dad read it to us when we were little."

"My Debbie used to love it, too." Hank reached for his handkerchief and blew his nose.

"It's okay, Grandpa," Karen said. "You still have us, right?"

"Yep," the man agreed. "I don't know what I'd do without you."

Joe looked across the room at Sylvie. She would be gone in a few days and they would go back to life the way it was before, without fresh bread and chicken casseroles and sugar cookies. His bed still held the faint scent of baby powder. Last night the sheets had been cold without her body next to his. Sylvie met his gaze and they looked at each other for a long moment until Hank's voice intruded.

"Well?" The old man frowned at him. "You reading or daydreaming?"

Joe opened the book. "'Twas the night before Christmas,'" he began, and pushed his memories aside.

"I'M GOING TO LEAVE this whole Santa Claus job to you young folks," Hank said. He yawned and reached for his jacket. "Besides, I need my beauty sleep since I have a date tomorrow."

"You'd better watch out," Joe said, pulling the cookie platter closer to him.

"Why?"

"I've seen the way Ruby Dee smiles at you, Hank." Joe chuckled and reached for the last sugarcoated reindeer. "If you're not careful, you're going to be a married man again."

"Hell." Hank looked over at Sylvie. "You know my heart belongs to you, don't you, honey?"

Sylvie, up to her elbows in soapy dishwater, could only shake her head. "Don't get me involved in this. I like Ruby. You two make a nice couple."

"I don't know if she can cook."

Sylvie laughed. "I don't know if I'd be fussy, if I were you."

"Look at it this way," Joe said. "You'll never have to pay for a haircut again."

"I don't have enough hair left to cut."

"I'm glad you invited her for dinner," Sylvie said.

"Well, honey, I am, too. I hate to see anyone spending Christmas Day all by themselves." Hank pulled on his jacket and grabbed his hat.

Joe got up and put his dirty dishes on the counter. "She doesn't have any family?"

Hank shrugged. "I guess it's kind of a sensitive subject, if you know what I mean." He turned to Sylvie. "You didn't forget those creamed onions, did you?"

"Of course not. You think I want to get fired on Christmas Day?"

The old man surprised her by stepping over and taking her into his arms for a hug. "You're a good girl, Sylvie. I'm sure glad you answered that ad."

"Me, too," she managed to reply.

Hank released her and headed for the back door. "Don't stay up too late, now. Those kids will be awake at the crack of dawn."

Joe followed him to the door. "You want me to call you when we get up?"

"Yep. I hate to miss any of the fun."

"Good night, Hank," Sylvie called. "Merry Christmas!"

"Merry Christmas," he replied, and the door banged shut behind him.

Joe turned to Sylvie. "You need any help?"

She rinsed the last mug and set it on the drainer to dry. "I'm done."

"Then I guess we'd better get the presents."

We? Sylvie glanced toward him as she dried her hands on the dish towel. "You want my help?"

"I'd appreciate it, yes. Seeing how Hank's bailed out on me this year."

"Where are the presents?"

"Out in the slaughterhouse. You go upstairs and make sure those little rascals are asleep and I'll start bringing things in." He reached for his coat. "And Sylvie?"

"Yes?"

"Thanks."

"For what?"

"You were right about Christmas. The, uh,

kids needed someone like you around to make it nice for them."

"You're welcome." She folded the towel neatly and set it on the counter. He was grateful for the help with the kids. Well, that was something. A man who said thank-you.

"SYLVIE," JANIE whispered, leaning over the bed. "I hear Santa downstairs."

Sylvie opened her eyes and blinked. "What?"

"I hear Santa."

"What time is it?"

"I dunno."

Sylvie couldn't have been sleeping long. It had taken an hour to get the presents arranged under the tree, another two hours to feed a suddenly fussy Dillon, and it was after one by the time she'd crawled into bed and drifted off to sleep. "Can you read the numbers on the clock?"

"'Four. One. Three.'"

Four-thirteen. She tried not to groan. "That's a little early for Santa, honey." She drew back the blanket. "Why don't you crawl in here with me for a little while?"

"'Kay. For a minute." Janie scrambled under the covers, her cold toes seeking the warmth of Sylvie's feet. "I hope I got a baby."

"Mmm," Sylvie said, closing her eyes. She'd rearranged the space under the tree so the big box that held Janie's doll was in the middle, clearly visible to an excited five-year-old. Joe, careful not to touch her during the hour they worked together, had made three trips outside to retrieve the toys.

"And a pony." She snuggled into Sylvie's shoulder. "And new colors. And pretty purple..."

"Mittens," Sylvie whispered, then joined the child in sleep.

HE HAD NO RIGHT TO watch her, but he couldn't resist. Karen and Peter were in Peter's room looking at what Santa had put in their stockings, but Janie had disappeared. He should have known she'd have found Sylvie. And he envied the child that spot in the bed beside the woman he couldn't love.

Her hair was a mess, which was all he could see since the rest of her was buried under blankets. The baby slept peacefully in his little bed right now, but Joe had heard Dillon giving his mom a hard time until almost one. He'd stopped himself from offering help. He didn't want to end up making love to Sylvie again. He couldn't lose control like that again.

"Sylvie," he whispered, unwilling to step into the room. When she didn't waken, he had no choice but to creep across the bedroom like a burglar and hover over the bed. "Sylvie," he tried again, but Janie was the one who opened her eyes.

"Santa came?" she asked, immediately wide awake. "Did I miss it?"

"You haven't missed a thing," he assured her.

"There's something by your bed and Karen's in with Peter."

"My stocking!" Janie scrambled out of the bed, accidentally kicking Sylvie awake, and was out the door in a matter of seconds. Without thinking what an intimate gesture it was, Joe sat on the edge of the bed.

"Merry Christmas," he said, wanting to lean over and kiss her as she gazed up at him through sleepy eyes.

"Is it morning?"

"It's about five-thirty." He wanted to brush the hair away from her cheek. He wanted to crawl into that warm bed and hold her body against his. And he wanted to remove that shabby T-shirt she wore as a nightgown and toss it into the trash. If she were his, they would go to bed naked every night.

But she wasn't his. And that was fine with him, Joe reminded himself. "Time to get up," he said, moving off the bed. "Did you set the coffee timer last night?"

She yawned—a tiny, feminine yawn—and snuggled into her pillow. "Um," was all she said, closing her eyes again. Joe didn't want to touch her in order to wake her again. He was too smart for that.

He raised his voice. "*Sylvie.*"

"Shh," was her only response, and that was with her eyes shut.

Dillon howled for breakfast, so Joe scooped him up. He was a cute little kid most of the time, but when he wanted to eat there was no shutting him up. "Your son wants to see what Santa brought. And he needs a clean diaper."

Sylvie struggled to sit up, revealing a tempting peek of cleavage and soft, pale skin. She pushed her hair out of her eyes. "I'm sorry," she said, stifling another yawn. "I fell back to sleep after Janie came in." She gave him a hesitant smile. "Merry Christmas."

"It's probably going to be different than the ones you're used to," he warned, suddenly curious about her family and why she wasn't with them today.

"Very different," she said. "Do you want me to take him?"

"Put on a robe or something and meet us in the kitchen. We'll wait for you and Dillon before we go into the living room." He handed her the damp bundle of baby, who immediately stopped fussing when held by his mother.

"I'll change Dillon and be right down. He can have his breakfast while the children open their presents."

"Sure." He hesitated, wanting to say something. Anything. He wanted to let her know that he was glad she was here, for the kids' sake, of course. And that he was sorry about the other night, even though he found it hard to be sorry about making love to her. Joe took a deep breath while Sylvie waited for him to speak, then said the first words that popped into his head. "Did you set the timer on the coffeepot last night?"

HANK HADN'T MEANT TO make the woman cry. "There, there," he said, watching helplessly as

Sylvie reached for another tissue and wiped her eyes. "It's just a little thing."

"No, it's not," she said, sliding the delicate silver bracelet onto her wrist. "It belonged to your wife and that makes it very special."

"She would have wanted you to have it," he assured Sylvie, hoping like heck he was saying something that would make her stop weeping like someone who'd had her heart broken in half.

"Thank you, Hank." She stepped over a pile of wadded-up wrapping paper and kissed him on the cheek. "I'll treasure it always."

"And I'll sure enjoy those cinnamon rolls," he told her before he looked toward the grandchildren. "Karen, honey, that kitten of yours is trying to climb up the tree again."

"Here, kitty," Karen said, stepping over unwrapped gifts. She grabbed the cat and looked down. "Sylvie, here's one for you. A big one."

"Maybe you'd better open it," Joe said, his voice suspiciously casual. Hank noticed that Joe couldn't take his eyes off their pretty little housekeeper as she carefully unwrapped some fancy silver paper tied with a big blue bow.

"Oh," Sylvie breathed, raising the lid of the box. "It's so beautiful." She reached inside and lifted out an ivory sweater, one of those things ladies wore that looked as soft and fuzzy as a new chick.

"Is it from Santa?" Janie asked, her new doll tucked in her arms.

Peter looked over a mountain of cardboard boxes. "Or from Grandpa?"

"There wasn't a card." Sylvie looked at Hank, who nodded toward Joe.

"You can take it back if it doesn't fit," Joe said gruffly.

Sylvie touched the sweater with reverent fingers. "I love it. Thank you."

"Uh, you're welcome."

Hank was pretty darn intrigued. So Joe was tired of that old sweater Sylvie wore all the time, and for Joe to spend money on a woman—well, that took some doing.

Maybe this would work out after all. For all of them.

He would have to start paying a little closer attention. Maybe if the young people spent more time alone together, there'd be fresh cinnamon rolls on the Rocky T for the rest of his life.

11

"My goodness," Ruby said, surveying the toys spread all over the living-room floor. "Santa was sure good to the Brockett family this year."

"What did Santa bring you?" Janie gave her a hug, and only Joe noticed that the woman's hand shook when she patted the little girl's back and that her smile looked a little forced.

"Well, I got some lovely flowers and some bath powder," she said. "And I see you have a beautiful new baby doll. What's her name?"

"It's a boy. Dillon, like Sylvie's baby."

"Well, he looks like he's a good baby." Ruby smiled at Joe, who was trying to figure out why women liked babies so much. "They both do. Dillon looks very comfortable with you."

Joe glanced down at the kid in his arms. Dillon was sound asleep, now that Sylvie had fed him again. He slept so quietly that every once in a while Joe jostled him a little, just to make sure he was breathing. "I guess he's had enough of Christmas for a while."

"I like your sweater," Karen said to Ruby. "It kinda matches my kitten." Sitting cross-legged on the floor, she held up the tiny animal. "Her name is Snowflake."

"Let me get you something to drink," Joe offered, as Ruby gingerly took the kitten. Her red-and-green sweater was fringed with fluffy white stuff that actually did look like that damn cat's fur. "Beer, wine, coffee, whiskey?"

"Wine would be nice, thanks." She held the kitten up to eye level. "She won't pee on me, will she?"

Karen hovered beside her new pet. "Only if she gets scared. Grandpa said she's afraid of his old dog and one time she wet all over his kitchen rug. He hid her at his house, but Sylvie got her in town. She was the last one left!"

"Well," Ruby said, handing her back to Karen. "What a nice gift she is. I got my son a dog one Christmas, and the darn thing ate half the sugar cookies, right off the plate."

Janie giggled. "Did you get mad?"

"Oh, I couldn't get mad at a puppy." She followed Joe into the kitchen, with the children trailing behind. "Sylvie, let me help with something."

"It's all done," Sylvie said, her cheeks flushed from the heat of the stove. "Oh, good, he's asleep," she said to Joe. "I'll take him up to bed."

Joe put the baby in her arms. He pretended he didn't notice that his fingers grazed her breast. He turned to Ruby. "White or red?"

"Whatever you have open is fine with me."

"Sylvie?"

"White, please. I'll be right back."

Joe heard Hank kicking the snow off his boots by the back porch. "Here comes your date."

Ruby's face lit up, but she joked, "I thought I'd been stood up."

"He went home to get the little house he made for Snowflake." Joe raised his voice so Hank could hear. "You know how hard it is at his age to remember things."

Hank stuck his head in the door. "I heard that," he grumbled. "You make me sound old."

"Aw, Hank," Ruby said, giving him a kiss on the lips. "You're not the least bit old. Merry Christmas, darlin'."

He grinned. "Well, I guess I'm getting younger by the minute."

Ruby reached up and rubbed a trace of rose lipstick from the corner of his mouth. "There," she said, smiling into his eyes as if they shared a secret. "That's better."

Joe forgot he was supposed to be pouring wine. Hank was getting kissed, he was holding babies, and homemade apple pies sat on the counter. Things had sure changed on the Rocky T.

SYLVIE WANTED TO SLOW everything down, to stretch the day into an endless, perfect time that would never finish. She'd seen a movie a few years ago where the people relived the same day over and over again. She wanted that.

Instead, she took pictures throughout the day. She'd finished her second roll of film before dinner, so she would have every special moment captured forever, like the television commercials promised.

"Smile," she said, when Hank opened his gift from Ruby and held up a pair of leather work gloves.

"Hold still," she said, when the children showed Dillon the little kitten and the baby's eyes widened with surprise.

"Look over here," she told Joe, who lay sprawled on the rug while teaching Peter a new board game.

"Your turn." Joe held out his hand for the camera. "You and Dillon stand by the tree."

Yes, she thought, that was exactly what she wanted to remember: Joe wearing the plaid shirt she'd ironed for him, Ruby and Hank teasing each other about dancing on New Year's Eve, the children with their endless enthusiasm and unending appetites, the platter of thumbprint cookies that made Hank hug her. She smiled for the camera.

Joe snapped the picture. "Why aren't you wearing your new sweater?"

"I didn't want to spill anything on it when I was cooking," she fibbed. She planned to return it and use the money for her trip back to Nebraska. She'd spent more on Christmas gifts than she'd planned, despite Hank's generous salary.

"Aren't you through cooking?" He stepped closer to hand her the camera.

"Well, yes, but I wanted to save it."

Joe frowned. "For what?"

"For when Dillon wouldn't spit up on my shoulder. For a special occasion."

"This isn't special enough?" he teased, a slight smile lighting his eyes.

"Why are you being nice?"

"It's Christmas," he said, as if that explained everything. "Come on, Sylvie, give me the baby and go put the new sweater on. I want to see that it fits."

"It will fit."

"Then put it on and I'll take a picture," he insisted. "I've never bought clothes for anyone before and I'm going to be nervous until I make sure you like it."

"I love it!" How could he think otherwise?

"Then put it on. Show Ruby I have some taste." He grinned and held out his arms for Dillon, so she had no choice but to hand over her fussy son.

"He's not in a very good mood," she warned.

"I'll give him to Ruby if he cries. She can play grandmother for a few minutes." He glanced toward the older woman and then back at Sylvie. "I wonder where her family is. I thought she had children somewhere."

"Everyone has a right to their own secrets," Sylvie said, backing up a step.

"The way you keep yours?" He lowered his voice so she could barely hear him. "Your parents aren't 'painting in Paris,' are they, Sylvie?"

She lifted her chin and looked him in the eye. "I don't have any parents—in Paris or anywhere else that I know of. I was abandoned when I was three, put in foster care until I was eighteen, and have made my own way ever since."

"I'm sorry."

"I don't want your pity."

"I meant, I'm sorry I asked. It wasn't any of my business." With his free hand he touched her shoulder. "Humor me, sweetheart, and let me see what you look like in it."

Sweetheart? Sylvie retrieved the sweater from its protective nest of white tissue and carefully folded it in her arms. It looked like the one in the window of Carol's Casuals—all fluffy and expensive. She would hate to return it, but there really wasn't any reason for her to own something so impractical. Except…Joe had picked it out for her, which was one more Christmas miracle she didn't know how she was ever going to forget.

HE COULD FORGET A LOT of things, but making love with Sylvie wasn't going to be one of them, no matter how hard he tried. Joe poured himself a glass of his best whiskey from the bottle he saved for special occasions. Last time he'd opened this particular bottle had been the afternoon that Janie was born. Deb hadn't had an easy time of it, so when he and Jim toasted the new little Brockett, there'd been tears of relief in their eyes.

"Son," Hank said, coming up behind him, "I'm gonna follow Ruby home. It's starting to snow." His eyebrows rose when he saw the whiskey on the kitchen counter. "What's going on, here?"

"Can't a man have a drink?"

Hank shook his head. "Asking her to stay on would be a lot easier than getting drunk."

"I'm not getting drunk and I don't know what you're talking about." Joe took a sip of his drink, but it didn't have the warming effect he'd hoped for. He still felt cold and he still wanted Sylvie—especially after he'd seen her in that sweater. He didn't know how a woman could look sexy and angelic at the same time, but Sylvie managed to do it.

Hank grabbed his coat. "She told me she's leaving tomorrow, like we agreed. I paid her the rest of what I owed her."

"That's your business."

"She's putting the kids to bed now. They're plumb worn-out. Ruby's up there saying goodnight."

"I'm glad you decided to ask her to spend Christmas with us."

"Well, she doesn't have any family around here, so it seemed like a good idea." He winked at Joe. "Don't wait up for me."

Joe stared back. "What?"

"Hey, I'm not dead yet. There's still some life in—"

"Hank?" Ruby entered the kitchen and put her empty glass in the sink. "You ready?" She turned to Joe. "Thanks again for a wonderful day, Joe. You all were real nice to share your family with me."

"We're glad you came, too, Ruby. I'll be by to get a haircut one of these days." He'd thought those gift certificates were a joke until he'd seen how tickled Sylvie and the girls were with them.

"I figured that would be more useful than a fruitcake." She laughed. "Stop by anytime and say hi."

"Sure."

Hank helped Ruby with her coat and put a protective arm around her shoulder when he led her out the door. So the old man had a girlfriend. There was no telling when he'd get home tonight, *if* he came home tonight. Hell. Hank wasn't shy about dating and Joe knew damn well that Hank had loved his wife. So why was it so hard for him? Had he become so used to his own grief that he couldn't even try to be happy anymore? That thought scared him, and Joe didn't like to be scared. And he didn't like to think of himself as a man who couldn't get on with his life, either.

Joe refilled his glass and wandered through the empty first floor. Someone—Sylvie, most likely—had picked up the living room and arranged the toys under the tree, which still had its lights blinking. She'd left two garbage bags stuffed with wrapping paper in the corner for him to take out. And someone had lit a fire in the fireplace, so the room smelled like pine. He sat on the couch and took another sip of the most expensive drink he'd ever had. And waited for Sylvie to come downstairs and keep him company.

He didn't like feeling so lonely—like he needed her or anything like that. But his heart started pounding faster when she walked into the living room and he noticed she still wore the new sweater.

"Do you want a drink?" he asked.

"No." She sat down on the couch beside him, which was odd. She usually picked a spot across the room from wherever he was. She even kicked off her slippers—the ones the kids had given her—and curled her feet up underneath her while she stared at the Christmas tree. "Would you do something for me?"

"Sure." The whiskey made him generous.

She didn't look at him. "Could we pretend…"

"Pretend what?"

Sylvie turned slowly to face him. "It's been the perfect day." He waited, knowing that women didn't like to be interrupted when they thought they were saying something important. "I've been pretending this is my family," she confessed, color flushing her pale skin. "And that this is my house. Pathetic isn't it? I hope your sister-in-law wouldn't mind."

"I know she'd be glad someone has been taking care of her children," he assured her, and realized he meant it. If Deb wouldn't mind having Sylvie in his house, why should he?

"I'm leaving tomorrow. I'm going to head back to Nebraska, see if I can get my old job back."

"All right," he said slowly.

"I've been listening to the weather forecast."

She smiled ruefully. "I don't want to get stuck in another storm."

"No." He didn't like the idea of her and Dillon setting out alone like that, in the middle of the winter, but he didn't have any right to protest. Despite everything, the woman was almost a stranger. He'd only known her for ten days. "Is there anything I can do to help?"

"You can go to bed with me tonight."

Joe stared. "I was thinking more along the lines of checking the antifreeze in your car."

"That, too."

"Why?" Which was a stupid question to ask, he realized. Especially since he remembered the other night all too well. It had been good. For both of them.

"The truth?"

"Yeah. That would help."

"I just wanted to be part of this…a little while longer. Neither one of us is thinking about love, but we're both alone." She smiled an upside-down smile. "And lonely, too. I guess I just wanted one more night before I go back to the real world."

"That's hard to resist." He leaned over and took her into his arms.

"Good." She snuggled against him and gazed at the tree. "When do we—you—take it down?"

"Anytime it doesn't interfere with football."

"Oh."

"Don't you want to know what team we root for?"

"I know what team *I* root for," she replied. "I live in Nebraska, remember?"

"I thought we were pretending," he whispered, moving her hair aside so he could kiss the back of her neck.

"I thought we were going to bed," she said, turning in his arms. He kissed her then, pretending nothing. He wanted her—more than he'd wanted her the first time. Tonight he knew what she tasted like against his mouth; he knew the enticing shape of her body and where she liked to be touched. He remembered the soft weight of her breast in his palm, the way he fit inside her, the soft sounds she made when she came.

He didn't have to pretend a damn thing.

Joe held her hand as they walked upstairs, but he resisted kissing her again until they were safely behind the locked door of his bedroom.

"Do we make love every night?" she whispered, her warm breath tickling his ear.

"Yeah, unless I've been lifting bales all day or you're asleep when I come to bed."

"You don't wake me?"

He shook his head and kissed her again. "Being a thoughtful man, I try to resist, but sometimes…in the morning…I run my hands under your nightgown, like this." His hands dipped beneath the hem of the white sweater and skimmed higher, to lift the sweater over her head. Sylvie caught it before it hit the floor. To Joe's amusement, she carefully draped it over a nearby chair.

"And then what?" she asked, turning back to him.

He led her to the bed. "It's better if I show you."

She stepped out of her jeans and, shivering, removed the rest of her underwear before she hurried into bed and drew the covers up over her bare skin. "Is it always this cold?"

"Sometimes I sleep with the window open," he admitted, removing his clothes even faster than Sylvie had. When he crawled between the cool sheets he was rewarded with the soft warmth of Sylvie's body next to his. He could get used to this, Joe realized; could grow accustomed to warmth and laughter and a woman's erotic scent. "Come here," he said, pulling her into his arms.

"As long as we're pretending," she said, "could we pretend that I have Cheryl Tiegs's body, too?"

"I like yours."

"Pretend I'm taller. And in really great shape," she said, laughter in her voice as she turned in his arms and his erection brushed her thighs.

"No," Joe replied, fitting himself between her legs when she parted her thighs. He rolled her onto her back and kissed her nose. "Your body's perfect just the way it is."

"A lovely lie," she said, and lifted her hips to let him enter, in a smooth stroke that made him think of heaven on earth. She was his, for tonight, and he would explore her body the way he longed to. He would take hours.

"Hours?" she said, running her hands down his back. He didn't know he'd spoken aloud.

"We have all night," he promised. "Don't we?"

She gasped as he thrust gently inside her, deeper this time, filling her slowly. "All night," she agreed, pulling him closer.

And later, while Sylvie lay asleep beside him in the darkness of his bedroom, after he'd gone downstairs to check the fire and unplug the tree lights, Joe drained the rest of his whiskey and realized he'd just experienced the best Christmas of his entire life.

12

"WHERE DID YOU GO?" Joe murmured, reaching for her across the bed.

"I fed Dillon," she whispered, sliding into the warm double bed and pulling the heavy covers up to her chin.

"Come here." He tugged her against him, fitting her neatly into the curve of his body. "Better?"

"Mmm. Much warmer." She put her cold toes on his leg, but he didn't jump.

"What's all this?" He plucked at her nightgown.

"I can't run around the house naked."

"Too bad." He nuzzled her neck. "What time is it?"

She closed her eyes and snuggled into the pillows. "Time for all good ranchers to get to work and quit fooling around with the help."

"Too early," he said, and from his quiet breathing Sylvie realized he'd gone back to sleep. She tried to stay awake for a while longer. She needed time to plan the day. She would be leaving, but not too early. Before lunch, perhaps. That way she could drive for five or six hours before stopping at a motel. She would go into

Willum to say goodbye to Ruby, pick up some disposable diapers and fill up the car with gas. She would keep the white sweater, though, even if she had to eat peanut butter for the next six months.

She'd never meant to fall in love, but she had. And she needed all the memories she could get.

"STAY," JOE SAID. She watched as he poured a cup of coffee and took it over to the kitchen table where she sat making a list of things to buy in town. It wasn't a very long list, but Sylvie thought she'd better write everything down, just in case.

"What?"

"Stay here. On the Rocky T."

"Stay," she repeated, unsmiling. He couldn't mean it. Or could he?

Joe sat down, facing her. "You and Dillon have a home here, if you want it." He reached over and plucked the pen out of her hand. "You don't have to go anywhere, unless you're still looking for whoever it was that made you come to Montana in the first place."

"Billy Ray Diamond," she managed to say, but she couldn't tell Joe that Billy Ray had pretended not to see her and his son. Some things were meant to be forgotten, and she would be working on this one for some time to come.

Joe shrugged. "Never heard of him."

"I wouldn't think so." Two very different men, two very different life-styles. What would

Joe have in common with an irresponsible rodeo cowboy? Except her.

"Hank said I should ask you to stay. Said it didn't make any sense for you to leave, not when we need you." He took her hand and absently played with her fingers. "And after last night, well, I got to thinking about that."

"You did?" She would have given the world to know what it was that he was asking. Was he offering her a job or a husband? A lover or a family? Sylvie took a deep breath. "I don't want you feeling sorry for me, Joe."

He looked surprised. "What? Hell, no, honey. I just don't want to lose you."

Do you love me? She waited to hear the words, but she didn't expect them—not from Joe. "You're offering me a job," she stated flatly.

"Not just a job," he said. "A home."

Sylvie gently pulled her hand away from his and tried to smile. "Thanks, Joe. I appreciate the offer, but I'm going to get back to my own life now."

"Your own life?" He frowned. "I don't get it."

"I've been living Deb Brockett's," she told him. She stood and gathered up her papers. "I've been pretending I'm her and so have you. So have her kids and her father. I've been living in her house and hanging up her Christmas ornaments and making cookies from her recipes. And last night I made love to the man who loved her. I've had enough pretending." Sylvie took a deep breath. "As screwed up as my own life is, it's time I got on with it. For everyone's sake."

"I can't..." He stopped.

"Love me?" she finished for him, and the stunned expression on his face told her she'd guessed right. "I know that, Joe. I never asked you to, remember?"

HE LOVED HER, ALL RIGHT. Almost since the first minute, when she'd come in from the storm and looked as if she might break in half. And when she'd scolded him for being a "grinch" about Christmas. And when he'd kissed her. And made love to her. And, last night, when he'd removed the white sweater and seen that she'd been so excited to wear something new, she'd forgotten to take the tags off.

He didn't want to love her. He'd thought he could only love one woman. Forever. No one else had appealed to him, excited him, until now. And he didn't want to need her or depend on her or...put his memories of Deb away. All Joe wanted to do was open that old bottle of whiskey again and forget about the damn "wife advertisement," once and for all.

"MEN ARE IDIOTS," Ruby declared, herding Sylvie and Dillon into the Hair Hut. She put the Closed sign in the window and locked the front door. "There," she said, leading Sylvie to her apartment in the back of the store. Sylvie blinked. She hadn't expected Ruby's home to look like a room in an English country estate, complete with rose chintz cushions and mahogany antiques. "Tell me all about it, honey, and don't spare the details."

"You don't have any appointments today?"

"Not the day after Christmas. I just opened the shop in case anyone walked in. Guess until I saw you on the sidewalk, I didn't have anything better to do. Sit down over there on the couch and take your coat off." She went over to the sink and filled a kettle with water. "I'm going to make us some tea and you're going to tell me why you were crying in front of Carol's store." She set the kettle on the stove and turned it to high. "I know her prices are ridiculous, but I've never seen anyone in tears about overpriced jeans before."

"It was the sweater. I was going to return it, after all." Joe's gift was still in the paper bag by her feet.

"Why? I thought it fit you real nice."

"The money would have come in handy on the trip home."

"Money isn't everything, honey. Sometimes looking good is half the battle. Here, give me that boy of yours." Sylvie unhooked the baby pack and Ruby scooped Dillon into her arms. "He's sleeping like an old bear in January, isn't he."

"It's the fresh air." Sylvie took a deep breath and fought another onslaught of tears. She'd cried all the way to town after saying goodbye to Hank and the children. There'd been nothing to say to Joe, but he'd given her a pat on the back and nodded. She hadn't expected anything more.

"You're leaving Joe," Ruby declared, sitting beside her on the flowered sofa and tucking Dillon into her lap. "Why? Doesn't he know he's in love with you?"

"He's not. He asked me to stay on as housekeeper."

"Let me guess. You two have been sharing the same bed?"

"Only twice."

"He's a fool." Ruby sighed. She handed the baby back to Sylvie as the teakettle whistled. "But a handsome one. I don't think he's a man used to loving."

"Or being loved in return," Sylvie added, thinking of Hank's daughter. "So it's best that I leave, before I get my heart broken again."

Ruby looked at Dillon. "His father didn't stick around, I guess."

"No. He's gone on to greener pastures…a woman with a cattle ranch and money to burn, I think. A short-order cook in North Platte couldn't hold his interest for long."

"Pardon me, honey," Ruby said, setting china cups on the highly polished tea table. "But you need a lift."

"What do you mean?"

"I mean, a new look." She leaned over and touched Sylvie's hair. "A good cut, some blond highlights, some makeup. Why don't you spend the night—I've got an extra bedroom in the back—and let me work miracles? That way, when you head out of here you'll look like a whole new woman."

Sylvie felt the first stirrings of hope. "'Miracles'? I think that's what it would take."

"I'll be right back." Ruby went into the beauty parlor and returned with a stack of magazines. "You drink your tea and look through these hairstyle books, then we'll decide just how beautiful you want to be."

"I don't know," Sylvie hedged. "Are you sure?"

"Sure as rain, honey. When you leave town, you'll feel better about yourself. That's what hairdressers are for."

"All right. I'll do whatever you say."

Ruby clapped her hands and her bracelets jangled. "Oh, boy, are we going to have fun!"

"You don't have the brains God gave a chicken," Hank fumed. He slammed his coffee mug on the counter and refilled it with the worst brew either man had tasted in twelve days.

"What did you want me to do, marry her?"

"Yes, dammit." He paced back and forth in front of the refrigerator. "That's exactly what I figured you'd do, but I should've known better. You don't have the balls."

"What do balls have to do with it?"

"Everything," Hank said. "It takes courage to lay your heart out there for any little gal to stomp all over. So yours got stomped on once. So what?"

"I didn't—"

"You wanted to marry my daughter, too, a long time ago." Hank glared at him. "One disappointment's going to keep you a sorry-ass bachelor for the rest of your life?"

Joe glared at him. "It takes one to know one."

Hank raised his eyebrows. "Not anymore. I've decided to branch out a little, have a little fun."

"You're going to marry Ruby Dee?"

"I don't know. Mebbe we're both happy with the way things are now, but the point—" he pointed his finger at the younger man "—is that I'm not sitting around whining."

"I'm not—"

"You'd be a good father to that little boy of hers."

"And if she's still in love with his father?" Even saying it out loud hurt.

"Did you ask her if she was?"

"Well, no, but—"

Hank took Joe's jacket off its hook and held it out to him. "You get your ass to town and make an honest woman of that girl or I'll take my grandchildren and move to town."

"This isn't any of your business, Hank." Joe felt so weary he could have crawled under the table and fallen asleep, but he took the jacket and tossed it on a nearby chair. He wasn't going anywhere—at least, not right away. "Besides, Sylvie's not in Willum. She's probably halfway home by now."

"According to my sources she's still here," the old man declared. "And for your information, young man, it *is* my business if my grandchildren are unhappy, and they've been cryin' since Sylvie drove out yesterday morning." He dumped the rest of his coffee into the sink. "I can't drink this stuff."

"I'm not going to get married just because you want good coffee and the kids want a mother." Joe rested his head in his hands and stared at the tabletop.

"Who said you should? You looked at yourself in the mirror lately? It's a pretty bad sight." Hank pulled out a chair and sat down. "Look, son," he said, clearing his throat. "All those years you couldn't tell my Deb how you felt about her... Well, I think you got in the habit of, uh, keeping your mouth shut. You know what I mean?"

"Not really." Joe's head was pounding. He should never have drowned his sorrows last night. He was old enough to know better.

Hank didn't seem ready to stop giving advice. "When you love a woman—if she isn't married to someone else—you ought to be man enough to shout it from the top of the barn, you know what I mean? It's not like it's shameful or nothing. Why, that's just part of being a man."

"I thought I'd always love Deb."

"And I loved my Laura. But we're alive, son. No one knows how much time we've got left on this earth, and with living comes loving."

"It's not that simple."

"Yes, it is. Not a day goes by that I don't miss my wife. And my daughter. And my son-in-law,

too. But I feel lucky to have my grandchildren."
Hank paused to pull out a handkerchief and
blow his nose. "And I'm damned lucky to have
found a woman who makes me laugh and
makes me glad to be alive. And so are you. Love
doesn't come along often, son. You've got to
grab it when it does."

"I've got to get some air." Joe stood, grabbed
his jacket and headed for the door.

"If you want to save some time," Hank called
after him, "you'll head right to the Hair Hut."

Joe didn't bother to answer. He wasn't going
to town. He was just going to get into the Jeep
and drive down the road and...check fence.
Yeah, that was what he would do. And if he *did*
happen to end up in town, it wouldn't be to find
Sylvie.

By the time he'd driven to the outskirts of Willum, Joe realized that finding Sylvie was exactly
what he wanted to do. He needed to know if the
damn woman was okay. It wasn't right for her
and that baby to be on their own, all alone in the
world. Hell, he'd never even gotten an address
so the kids could write to her.

He didn't really know what he would say
when he saw her. "Come back" probably
wouldn't do it. He'd have to be more convincing, but the thought of trying to say what was in
his heart only made his stomach clench up in
knots. He sure as hell had never told any woman
that he loved her. Sylvie might not listen to him.
She might not even talk to him. While he
couldn't imagine climbing on a rooftop and an-

nouncing his intentions to the world, Joe drove toward Main Street knowing he had to think of something. Fast.

SYLVIE GAZED OUT THE shop window toward Main Street. "It looks as if it's going to snow again."

Ruby looked up from the latest issue of *People* magazine. "Guess I should close up soon. Business isn't going to pick up until right before New Year's Eve. Do you want to go over to the café for dinner tonight?"

"Sure, when Dillon— Uh-oh." She rubbed condensation off the glass and looked again. Sure enough, that was Joe's Jeep pulling into a parking space in front of the café. He didn't get out right away. His head was down, as if he was reading, but in a few minutes he stepped out of the car and buttoned his coat. She wondered what he was doing in town. Surely he couldn't know she was still here. She watched as he frowned up at the sky, then looked across the street at the window of the Hair Hut.

"What on earth's got your attention?"

"Joe's in town. Did you tell Hank I was here?"

"I may have mentioned it." Ruby tossed the magazine aside and hurried over to the window. "He's heading this way. Oops. He should've watched out for that puddle."

"Why would he come here?"

"For you, honey. Why else?"

"Maybe he wants a haircut." She turned to see Ruby heading for the apartment door. "Don't leave me alone with him! I don't want to make a fool of myself."

Ruby sighed and picked up a broom. "Okay, I'll sweep for a few minutes, but I'm going to stay as far away from the two of you as I possibly can."

"Thanks," Sylvie said, and the door opened to admit one very large rancher who looked tired and pale. "What's the matter with you?" The words were out before she could take them back.

"Nothing a good night's sleep won't cure." He pulled a piece of paper out of his pocket, then stared at her. "What did you do to your hair?"

Sylvie tucked her blond-highlighted chin-length hair behind one ear. "Do you like—" She stopped. "I had a makeover."

"You were fine the way you were."

"Thank you, but I think this is more sophisticated." She saw him take in the ivory sweater, the fashionably faded jeans that had once belonged to Ruby, and the wide silver bracelet that graced one wrist. Ruby had given her makeup samples: delicate rose blusher, glossy lipstick and a sheer, pink nail polish. She was a new woman, ready for a new life.

"Why do you want to be sophisticated?"

"Maybe I don't want to be a cook forever."

"What do you want to be?"

"I don't think that's any of your business," she replied, pleased with herself for standing up to him. She didn't know what he was doing here at Ruby's, but if he'd come to offer her the housekeeping job again, he could just go back to where he came from. "Why are you here, Joe? What do you want?"

He continued to stare at her. "I've been thinking," he said slowly, "I'm not very good at pretending."

"You were the other night." Her face grew warm as she remembered his body inside hers. She glanced at the sheet of paper in his hand. "What's that? Another ad for a wife?" It was a bad joke, she knew, because Ruby groaned and then coughed as if she hoped they hadn't heard her.

"As a matter of fact, it is," Joe said. He looked over toward the back of the shop. "Hi, Ruby."

"Hi, Joe." Ruby leaned on the broom and waited to see what would happen next. She looked at Sylvie and shrugged as if to say, *How would I know what he's talking about?*

"An ad for a wife?" Sylvie thought it must be some kind of joke and held out her hand. "For who?"

"For me."

"Why? Tired of drinking your own coffee already?"

He tried to smile. "That's part of it."

"Let me see." She held out her hand.

Joe glanced at Ruby. "Ruby, would you mind giving us some privacy?"

"Sure," she said, sweeping toward the apartment door.

"I want Ruby to stay," Sylvie declared. That

way, she wouldn't be alone with Joe. Because whenever she was alone with the rancher, she ended up kissing him. Or worse. And now, just seeing him made her want to go right into his arms and never leave. And leave was exactly what she needed to do.

"Honey, are you sure?" Ruby looked as if she wanted to take the baby and run. "I think you and Joe have a lot to say to—"

"Joe can talk to me here." *And I can keep at least a foot between his body and mine at all times.*

"I'm real specific," Joe warned before giving the ad to her to read.

Sylvie turned the paper around and gazed at the uneven printing, but it took her a few seconds to concentrate on the words.

"Not just anyone will do," Joe added, taking a step closer. "As you can see, she has to promise to sleep with me every night and only yell at me once a day, and she has to think about letting me adopt her son."

Sylvie's hand shook when she handed the paper back to him, but her voice was steady. "You're going to have a hard time finding someone, Mr. Brockett."

Joe stood his ground. "I ran out of room on the page before I got to the most important part."

She waited.

"She has to let me tell her how much I love her. Every morning and every night. And even if she still loves that other man, the one before me—what was his name?"

"Billy Ray," Sylvie supplied.

"Billy Ray?" Ruby gasped and the broom fell to the floor with a loud bang. *"Billy Ray Diamond?"*

Sylvie turned to stare at her. "Yes. Do you know him?"

"Wait just a minute," Ruby said, moving to take a protective stance beside the playpen where Dillon slept, peacefully unaware that his mother was in the middle of receiving a marriage proposal. "I know him, all right. You mean to tell me that I'm a *grandmother?*"

For a long moment Sylvie couldn't say a word, but the stricken expression on Ruby's face could mean only one thing. She ignored Joe, who was looking back and forth between the two women. "You're Billy Ray's mother?"

Ruby nodded and pulled a tissue from her pocket. "Yes, for what it's worth."

"But your last name…"

"I got pretty tired of all the jokes that came from being named 'Ruby Diamond.'" She tried to smile, but failed miserably. "I should never have married that man, but I was in love and not too smart, if you know what I mean. And then Billy Ray came along and I was busy trying to keep food on the table and care for my son."

"He was here. In town."

Ruby didn't look surprised. "He called me a few days ago, but didn't leave a number." She sank into one of the hair-dryer chairs. Sylvie sat beside her and tried to control her feelings. Dillon had a grandmother. This was the biggest

Christmas gift she'd ever received. Dillon would have family.

But she had to tell Ruby the painful truth. "I saw him. With a woman. And I heard he was married."

Ruby's eyes filled with tears again. "Oh, sweetheart, I'm sorry for everything he's done to you. That boy of mine has been trouble since the day he turned thirteen."

Neither woman noticed that Joe had grabbed the manicurist's chair and placed it in front of them. "Pardon me, Ruby, but it doesn't seem to me that Billy Ray has any business being involved in Dillon's life." He glanced toward the sleeping baby. "Unless, later, when the boy's grown up and has questions." He turned to Sylvie. "Are you going to marry me or not?"

"If he didn't do the right thing by Sylvie, then he has no rights to the child." Ruby gave Sylvie a watery smile. "But I'd like to think you'd let me be his grandma."

Sylvie wiped her own eyes with the back of her hand. "You have to be a maid of honor first, Ruby." She turned to Joe. He didn't look as if he wanted a housekeeper. He looked like a man who hadn't slept.

And he looked like a man in love. She wanted to throw herself into his arms, but there was one question she had to ask first. "Do you love me?"

"More than anyone else in the world," Joe admitted. He smiled and took the crumpled sheet of paper from his coat pocket. "Either you say you're marrying me or I post this ad at Buttrey's to see if anyone shows up at the Rocky T."

"Forget it, Mr. Brockett," Sylvie said, going into his arms. "I'm taking the job."

Epilogue

KAREN HATED TO POST the advertisement, but she didn't have any other choice. Uncle Joe had put his foot down, and even Sylvie had sided with him this time. It wasn't fair. She stood in front of the bulletin board and looked for a good place to put the card. It had to be in just the right spot—preferably someplace that was hidden by an ad for vacuum cleaners or car insurance.

She tossed her hair over her shoulder and stalled for a few minutes more. Janie and Peter had gone with Sylvie to see Grandma Ruby, and as soon as Karen left Buttrey's she would go to the Hair Hut to get her nails done in time for Lindsey's thirteenth birthday party.

She found an unused thumbtack and stuck the card below a faded advertisement for income-tax preparation. Free Kittens, she'd been forced to print. To Good Homes Only. She'd added a phone number, but she had left out the information that white kittens were smart. There was no reason to give anyone an extra reason to take one of Snowflake's babies away from the Rocky T. And Uncle Joe would never know that Karen had printed a fake phone number on the card.

"Karen?"

She turned to see Sylvie walking toward her in her new red coat. "Yeah?"

"I was worried about you, so I came back." Sylvie gave her a tissue, but Karen refused it. She was angry, not sad. "I don't want to give the kittens away."

Karen watched as Sylvie peered at the neat printing on the index card. "Hmm. You always were good with ads," was all she said before leading Karen out of the store.

Karen grinned. Finding Sylvie was the best thing that had ever happened. Uncle Joe said it all the time, especially right after Sylvie made cinnamon rolls. And then there'd been their second Christmas as a family, with Sylvie telling everyone that there was going to be a new baby. Grandpa had cried and Grandma Ruby's eye makeup had run down her face.

"Sylvie?" She winced as the wind blew the breath back into her mouth.

"Yes?"

"What do you want for Christmas?"

"Nothing." Sylvie put her arm around Karen and gave her a hug. "I have everything I ever dreamed of."

Karen blinked back tears. Everyone knew she didn't cry. "Me, too."

HARLEQUIN®

Temptation

It's hotter than a winter fire.
It's a BLAZE!

In January 1999 stay warm with another
one of our bold, provocative, *ultra-sexy*
Temptation novels.

#715 *TANTALIZING*
by Lori Foster

It was lust at first sight—but Josie and Mark were both
pretending to be other people! They were giving new
meaning to the term "blind date." How to unravel the web
of deceit? And still hang on to that sexy stranger...

BLAZE!
Red-hot reads from Temptation!

Available wherever Harlequin books are sold.

HARLEQUIN®
Makes any time special ™

**WHEN THINGS START TO HEAT UP
HIRE A BODYGUARD...**

YOUR BODY IS OUR BUSINESS

Discreet, professional
protection

1·800·555·HERO

AND THEN IT GETS HOTTER!

There's a bodyguard agency in San Francisco where
you can always find a HERO FOR HIRE, and the man
of your sexiest fantasies.... Five of your favorite
Temptation authors have just been there:

JOANN ROSS *1-800-HERO*
August 1998
KATE HOFFMANN *A BODY TO DIE FOR*
September 1998
PATRICIA RYAN *IN HOT PURSUIT*
October 1998
MARGARET BROWNLEY *BODY LANGUAGE*
November 1998
RUTH JEAN DALE *A PRIVATE EYEFUL*
December 1998

HERO FOR HIRE
A blockbuster miniseries.

Available at your favorite retail outlet.

HARLEQUIN®

Temptation®

Look us up on-line at: http://www.romance.net   HTEHFH

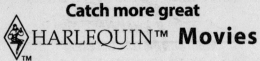

HARLEQUIN®

Temptation

He's strong. He's sexy.
He's up for grabs!

Harlequin Temptation and
Texas Men magazine present:

1998 Mail Order Men

#691 THE LONE WOLF
by Sandy Steen—July 1998

#695 SINGLE IN THE SADDLE
by Vicki Lewis Thompson—August 1998

#699 SINGLE SHERIFF SEEKS...
by Jo Leigh—September 1998

#703 STILL HITCHED, COWBOY
by Leandra Logan—October 1998

#707 TALL, DARK AND RECKLESS
by Lyn Ellis—November 1998

#711 MR. DECEMBER
by Heather MacAllister—December 1998

Mail Order Men—
Satisfaction Guaranteed!

Available wherever Harlequin books are sold.

HARLEQUIN®
Makes any time special ™

Look us up on-line at: http://www.romance.net   HTEMOM